Poul Anderson

Murder in Black Letter
(Thriller Classic)

OK Publishing 2021

Poul Anderson
Murder in Black Letter

(Thriller Classic)

Published by
MUSAICUM
Books

- Advanced Digital Solutions & High-Quality book Formatting -

musaicumbooks@okpublishing.info

2021 OK Publishing

ISBN 978-80-272-7361-4

Contents

To him whom I shall ever regard
as the best and wisest man whom
I have ever known

1

Steel talked between roses. Kintyre parried Yamamura's slash; his riposte thumped on the other man's arm.

"Touché!" exclaimed the detective. He took off his mask and wiped sweat from a long, high-cheeked face. "Or is it you who's supposed to say that? Anyhow, enough for today."

"You're not doing so badly, Trig," Kintyre told him. "And I have some revenge due for all those times you've had me cartwheeling through the air, down at the dojo."

Trygve Yamamura clicked his tongue. He stood over six feet tall, lanky, the Oriental half of him showing mostly in narrow black eyes and smoked-amber skin. "You would use sabers, wouldn't you?" he said.

Robert Kintyre shrugged. "A foil is for women and I'm not fast enough for an épée. Also, there's professional interest. A saber is a wee bit closer to the Renaissance weapon."

"I think I'll stick to Japanese swords."

Kintyre nodded. He was a stocky man of medium height, with straight dark hair above a square, snub-nosed, sallow-complexioned face. His eyes were gray under level brows, and set unusually far apart; there was little else to mark him out physically, until you noticed his gait. To an only slightly lesser degree than Yamamura's, it had the indefinable compactness of a judo man.

They stood in a garden in Berkeley. Walls enclosed them: the main house, now vacant while its owner and family were on vacation; the three-room cottage to the rear which Kintyre rented; a board fence strewn with climbing blossoms on either side. Overhead lay a tall sky where the afternoon sun picked out the vapor trail of a jet sliding above San Francisco Bay.

"I agree, Samurai swords make these look like pitchforks," said Kintyre. "But you can't do much with them except collect them. Too damned effective!"

Yamamura removed his padded coat and fished for his pipe. "You off work now?" he asked.

"Yep. Last bloody paper corrected, last report in, term's over, and I'm not teaching again till fall. It's great, though impoverished, to be free."

"You're making a pack trip into Kings Canyon, aren't you?"

"Uh-huh. Bruce Lombardi and I were supposed to leave tomorrow. Only what the devil has become of Bruce?" Kintyre scowled. "His girl called me last night, said he'd left the day before — Saturday — and hadn't come back yet. She was worried. I'm beginning to be."

"Hm." Attentiveness flickered up in Yamamura. His agency, small and new, had no engagements at the moment. However, he spoke with no more than friendly concern. "Is it like the kid to go tearing off that way? I don't know him especially well, he's just somebody I meet now and then at your place."

"That's the point," said Kintyre. "It is not like him. The department head inquired about it this morning. Bruce hasn't turned in the grades for two of his classes; and he's disgustingly reliable, normally." He paused. "On the other hand, he's having his troubles these days and — anyhow, I hesitate to —"

Footsteps sounded in the driveway. A trim quasi-military shape came around the house.

"Officer Moffat," said Yamamura. He had belonged to the Berkeley force until he set up for himself. "What's happened?"

"Hello, Trig," said the policeman. He turned to the other. "Are you Professor Robert Kintyre?"

"Assistant professor only, no cobwebs yet." Why did he answer with a bad joke, he wondered — postponing something?

"How do you do. I'm sorry to bother you, sir, but we're trying to identify a young man who was found dead this morning. I was told that someone of his description was a teaching assistant in the history department, and that you knew him best."

The voice was sympathetic, but Kintyre stood very quietly for a moment. Then: "I know a lot of young men, but perhaps — Bruce Lombardi?"

"That's the name I was given," said Moffat. "I'm told you were his faculty adviser."

"Yes." Kintyre pawed blindly after a cigarette, meeting only his jacket. "How did he come to die?"

"If it is him. Do you think you could identify him for us? I warn you, it isn't pretty."

"I've seen dead men before," said Kintyre. "Come on." He started toward the street.

"Your clothes," said Moffat gently.

"Oh, yes. Yes. Thanks." Kintyre fumbled at his equipment. He threw it on the grass. "Put this junk away for me, will you, Trig?" His voice was uncertain. "I'll call you later."

"Sure," said Yamamura in a low tone. "Call me anytime."

Kintyre followed Moffat to the police car. It nosed off the shabby-genteel residential street and into southbound traffic. Moffat, at the wheel, pointed to the cigarette lighter.

Kintyre put tobacco smoke into his lungs and insisted: "What happened?"

"He seems to have been murdered." Moffat's eyes flickered sideways along his passenger's wide shoulders, down to the thick wrists and hands. "We'll go to headquarters first, if you don't mind, and you can talk to Inspector Harries."

In the following time, at the office, Kintyre answered many questions. Inspector Harries seemed to have little doubt who his corpse was, but much uncertainty about everything else.

"Bruce Lombardi. Age twenty-four, did you say? Five feet nine, slender build, brown eyes, curly brown hair — m-hm. Did he wear glasses?"

"Yes. He was nearsighted. Horn rims."

"What kind of clothes did he ordinarily pick?"

"Anything he got his hands on. He was a sloppy dresser. I remember — no, never mind."

"Please tell me, Dr. Kintyre. It may have some bearing."

"Hardly. This was about five years ago. I was an assistant bucking for an instructorship, he was a freshman with a major in my department — history, did I tell you? There was some kind of scholastic tea or something — semiformal — you know. He showed up in a secondhand tweed jacket and an old pair of khaki wash pants. He honestly thought they were suitable for — Never mind. It seemed funny at the time."

Kintyre stubbed out his cigarette (the fifth, sixth, twentieth?) and took a deep breath. He was letting this run away with him, he thought. He was yattering like an old woman, shaken into brainlessness. It was not as if he had never encountered death before.

He groped toward the teaching of the dojo, the judo school. Judo is only in part a sport; it is also a philosophy, the Gentle Way, with many aspects, and the first thing to learn is to relax utterly. The passive man is prepared for anything, for he can himself become anything.

But it was an unreal attempt. Kintyre's interest in judo was a superficial growth of a few years; his roots lay in the West. He understood with sudden bleakness why Bruce's death had so clamped on him: once again someone he cared for was gone, and the horror he had borne for two decades stirred toward awakening.

"Don't you feel well, Dr. Kintyre?"

Harries leaned over the desk, politely concerned. "I'm sorry to put you to a strain like this. If you want to rest a while — "

"No." Kintyre mustered a degree of steadiness. "I was a bit shaken, but — Go ahead. If Bruce really was murdered, I certainly want to give you any help I can finding who did it."

The inspector regarded him thoughtfully. "You and he were pretty close, weren't you?"

"In a way. He was almost eleven years younger than I, and had lived a — limited life. Not sheltered in the usual sense, his family being poor, but limited. And he was such a peaceful fellow, and his life since entering college had been mostly books. It made him seem even younger."

Kintyre sighed. "We got to be about as friendly as one can get under such circumstances," he finished. "Maybe I looked on him as a son. Not being married, I can't be sure of that."

"Did he ever say anything which led you to believe that he might be in serious trouble?"

"No. Absolutely not. That is, I knew his older brother hung — hangs around with a dubious crowd over in San Francisco, and it distressed him, but he never implied anything really bad was involved."

"Let's see." Harries looked at some notes. "I gather he left his, uh, girl friend's place about six P.M. Saturday, telling her he had business over in the City and she shouldn't wait up. She got worried and checked with you Sunday evening. And he was found by a patrol car this morning, at daybreak, on the bank of the old frontage road, near the Ashby Avenue turnoff."

"You've worked fast," said Kintyre. *Or did I tell you all this?* he wondered. *There are a few minutes which I remember only hazily. I was so busy fighting myself.*

"What did you do over the weekend?" asked Harries in a casual tone.

"Oh, let's see — Saturday morning I puttered around down at the yacht harbor, doing some work on my boat. I went home in the afternoon, graded papers and so on, went out at night and had a few beers with a friend — Dr. Levinson of the physiology department. Sunday morning I took a sail on the Bay, and later finished my paperwork. Shortly after Miss Towne had called me, I was invited over to Gerald Clayton's suite at the Fairhill. We had some drinks and talked till quite late. This morning I turned in my last reports to the University, came home, and was horsing around with Trig Yamamura when your man arrived."

"You seem pretty well alibied," smiled Harries. "Not that we suspect anyone on this side of the Bay."

"Why not?"

Harries' mouth tightened. "Dr. Kintyre, you'll undoubtedly be asked a great many more questions in the next several days. Get the worst over with now. Then go out with some friends and have a lot more drinks. That's my advice."

They shook hands, feeling it was a somehow theatrical gesture, and thus being embarrassed without knowing how to avoid it. Moffat drove Kintyre through miles of city, down to that place in Oakland where the dead man was kept.

They entered a chill room. Kintyre took the lead, compulsively. He went to the sheeted thing and uncovered it.

After a while he turned around. "Bruce Lombardi," he said. "Yes."

"I'm sorry you — Oh, hell." Moffat looked away. "He was a sort of handsome young chap, wasn't he? Thin regular features and so on. I'll bet his parents were proud of him."

"They paid his undergraduate expenses," mumbled Kintyre. "Since then he went ahead on scholarships and assistantships, but those were four high-priced years for a poor family."

"And now they'll see this. Hell." Moffat stood with fingers doubled together, talking fast. He himself was rather young, more shaken than his superiors would have wished. "Look at those burns — marks — He's like that all over. He was never unconscious once, unless he passed out now and then — no blackjack marks, no chloroform, just rope bruises. Then when he was dead, the murderers cut off his fingers and hacked his face some more, to make it harder for us to identify. Stuffed him into an old coat and pair of pants and left him half in the tidewater. Twenty-four years of age, did you say? This is what the old Lombardis have to show for their twenty-four years. Jesus Christ. I'll bet *I* have to take his father in here."

"You think it was a sadist?"

"Oh, sure, I don't doubt at least one of the murderers got his kicks. It takes a cracked brain to do something like this — even for money. Yes, I feel pretty sure it was a professional job. Most of the torture was systematic, almost neat, for a definite purpose. You can see that. When they reached their purpose, when he talked or whatever it was, they cut his throat — neatly — then mutilated him for a good logical reason, to make it harder for us, and disposed of the body in regular gangland style. They shouldn't have dumped him in Berkeley. The Berkeley force sees so many University people we automatically thought a nice-looking young fellow like this might belong on the campus, and checked. But that was their only mistake. Mine was going in for a job where I'll have to show this to his father."

"Must you?"

"It's the law. I wish it weren't."

Moffat moved to pull back the sheet, but Kintyre was there first. Covering Bruce's face made a kind of finality. Though the real closing curtain had fallen hours ago, he thought, when Bruce lifted hands torn, broken, and burned, to take death for his weariness. And afterward they cut his fingers off. Maybe the curtain had not been rung down yet.

2

By the time Kintyre got back, it was close to sunset. He entered a book-lined living room. There were a few good pictures, a small record player, his sabers hung on the wall by Trig, the furniture bought used or made out of old boxes — otherwise little. He did not believe in cluttering life with objects.

He poured himself a stiff drink. Glenlivet was his only expensive luxury. He sat down to savor it and perhaps think a little about Bruce. There was no solid reason why the boy should have made so large a niche in Kintyre's existence, but somehow he had. The emptiness hurt.

When the phone rang, Kintyre was there picking it up before consciousness of the noise registered. He was not surprised to hear Margery Towne's voice.

"Bob? You know?"

"Yes. I'm sorry. I wish to hell I could tell you just how sorry."

"I can guess." Her tone was flattened by the control she must be keeping on it. "We both loved him, didn't we?"

"I think everybody did."

"Somebody didn't, Bob."

"I suppose you heard through the police?"

"They were here a few minutes ago. Do they know *everything?*"

"Probably I gave them your name. They came to me first, for the identification."

"They were very nice about it and all that, but — "

Silence whistled remotely over the wires.

"Bob, could you come talk to me? Now?"

"Sure, pony. Give me half an hour."

Kintyre hung up one-handed, starting to undress with the other. He went through a shower and put on a suit in ten minutes.

Margery's apartment was catercorner from his, with the University between. He parked his battered '48 De Soto on the near side of the campus and walked across, hoping to hoof out some of the muscular tightness and set his thoughts in order.

Level yellow light came through eucalyptus groves to splash on a cropped greensward and pompous white buildings, almost bare of mankind in this pause between baccalaureate ceremonies and summer classes. Kintyre reflected vaguely that he would have to go through Bruce's desk, finish his work, yes, and complete his study of the Book of Witches....His mind drifted off toward a worried practical consideration. What could he do about Margery?

He wanted to help her, if he could — double damnation, hadn't he tried before? At the same time he was not, repeat not, going to get himself involved. It would be unfair to both of them.

There were rules of the game, and so he had played it with her. You left wives and virgins alone: well, she was long divorced, and had slept around a bit since then. You neither gave to nor took from a woman. You made it perfectly clear you weren't interested in anything permanent. And when you broke it off, after a pleasant few months, you did it cleanly: he had the best excuse in the world, back in 1955, an academic grant that returned him to Italy for a year of research in his specialty, the Renaissance. (But she had been very quiet, the last few weeks; sometimes at night he had heard her trying not to cry.) Back home again, you didn't resume old affairs: you were simply friendly, on such occasions as you happened to meet.

Yes, of course. Only then she took up with Bruce, and Bruce had wanted to marry her, and she had plainly been considering it, and now Bruce was dead and Kintyre was on his way to console her. Could you walk in her door and say: "Hello, I still subscribe to the why-buy-a-cow philosophy so be careful, now you may weep on my shoulder"?

He realized he was sucking on a dead cigarette. He threw it away and stopped to light another. He was almost under the building which housed his own department.

"Good evening."

Kintyre looked up. Jabez Owens was walking toward him.

"Hello," he answered. "How are you? Excuse me, but I've got to — "

Owens reached him and took his hand. "My dear old chap," he said in his most Harvard accent, "I'm awfully sorry."

"Hm?"

"Young Lombardi. I saw it in the papers. You know?"

"Yes." Kintyre looked coldly at Owens. The writer was a tall man, the breadth of his shoulders attributable only in part to his tailor. He had straight ruddy features, dark wavy hair graying at the temples, blue eyes behind wrought-iron glasses, tweedy clothes with a scarf filling the V of the jacket, and a small calabash pipe in one pocket.

"I know he was murdered," said Kintyre, watching the other's face.

"Terrible. I remember once in Sumatra — but that was long ago. See here," said Owens candidly, "I know you know of my disagreements with the poor young fellow. Why, it was only — when? Thursday night we were at that party at Clayton's. You must have heard us quarreling over his silly thesis. But this! *De mortuis nil nisi bonum.*"

Kintyre did not like Owens. It was not so much the scholar raising his hackles at a rather lurid popularizer. What the devil, Owens' books stirred up some public interest; they passed on some information, however distorted; and that was more than you could say for the average historiographic monograph. But during the whole week he had been in Berkeley, one long theatrical performance had gone on, with Jabez Owens the plot, dialogue, director, producer, star, supporting cast, and claque. It grew monotonous.

Wherefore Kintyre said maliciously: "I'll be completing that thesis for him. Doubtless I too will be forced to include a side glance at those Borgia letters of yours. But it'll take me a while, I don't have all the facts and deductions at my fingertips as he did. So I suggest you hurry to Hollywood and get that movie started."

Owens laughed a well gauged laugh, neither too loud for this posthumous argument nor too small to sound genuine. "I'd love to take you on," he said. "Nothing I like better than a good verbal fight, and that's what the boy was giving me. As a matter of fact, I may be staying here a few more days. Or maybe not. But what I really stopped you for was to offer my sympathy and ask if I could help."

"What with?" asked Kintyre. It stuck him as a bit of a coincidence that Owens had happened to be passing by this special building at this moment.

"Oh, I don't know. Nothing, I suppose. You seem headed toward his, ah — " Owens paused delicately — "his fiancée's place. I gathered from someone's remark, she lives in this area."

"Uh-huh."

"Charming girl. Poor Lombardi. She is so good a reason for not dying. Please give her my regrets. Ah — a moment more, if you will."

"Yes?" Kintyre was turning to go; he stopped.

Owens flushed. "Don't misunderstand me. It's none of my business, certainly. But I'd say at a guess I am a good fifteen years older than you, and perhaps — I suppose I needn't advise you. But I do want to help you. And her. See here, take her out tonight. I know they were living together. There'll be too many memories at her home." He nodded, almost awkwardly. "Pardon me. I have to go now. I'll be seeing you."

Kintyre stared after him. *The deuce you say! I didn't think you had a genuine bone in your body.*

He glanced at his watch. He was late. His steps lengthened, a hollow noise on the sunset pavement.

Past the elaborate south gate, down a few shop-lined blocks of Telegraph Avenue, then left, slightly uphill, along a street of rooming houses and small apartments. Margery's flat was here; or should you say it had been Bruce's? He had gotten his mail, discreetly, at another address (which must now be overrun with sight-seers) — but this was Theirs.

Kintyre went upstairs. Margery opened her door at his buzz and closed it again behind him.

Bruce had moved in with her during the Christmas holidays, half a year ago now, but the interior was still hers, airily modern. Starting on bluff and nerve and a jerkwater college's art degree, she had made herself important to a local firm of decorators. Bruce would have lived happily in a cave, if it had had book-shelves.

And yet somehow, thought Kintyre as he waited for Margery to speak — somehow, she had reshaped the place around him. The piano he played so well stood tuned for him; by now, most of the records were ones which he had shown her — quietly, even unconsciously — were good to have. She had matted and hung one of his inkbrush sketches, a view from Albany Hill toward the Golden Gate, whose contours brought you back for a second look.

And, of course, nearly all the books were his, and she had made an offside room into a study for him. When you added it up, maybe only the clothes and the parakeet were altogether her own.

I never affected her like this, thought Kintyre. *Margery's apartments always felt nervous before. Somehow Bruce made this one peaceful.*

"Hello," he said, for she was evidently not going to speak first.

"Hi." She went over to a glass-topped coffee table and opened a cigarette box. "Thanks for coming."

"No thanks needed," he said. "Could be you'll help me more than I will you."

She looked at him for a moment, and he realized it had been a tactless answer with too many unwanted implications. But then she picked up a cigarette and flicked a lighter to it. "Drink?" she asked.

"Well — you drink too much, pony."

"Perhaps you don't drink enough," she said.

"I like the taste. I don't like being drunk."

"You're afraid to lose control, aren't you? Sometimes, Bob, I think that explains you. To you, life is a ride on a tiger, and you've got to keep the reins every minute."

"Let's have none of these bad amateur psychoanalyses," he said, following her into the kitchen. He came up behind her and laid his hands on her waist. "And let's not fight. I'm sorry, Marge. I'm sorry for Bruce and for you."

Her head bent. "I know, Bob. Don't bother with words." She put the cigarette to her lips, took a puff of smoke, blew it out, lowered the cigarette, and twisted about between his hands. Her lips brushed his cheek. "Go on, I'll mix. I want to keep busy."

He returned to the living room and prowled out his unrest for a few minutes. The piano caught his gaze, he saw ruled bescribbled sheets and went over to look. Margery found him thus, when she came in with two glasses. "Sit down," she invited.

He regarded her through careful eyes, trying to judge her needs — and her demands, for his own warning. She was a trifle on the short side, her figure was good though tending to plumpness, and even he could appreciate the effect of her simple green dress. Her face was broad, with a slightly pug nose, very full lips, blue eyes under arched brows, a few freckles: "pert" was the word. Reddish hair fell in a soft bob just below the ears, which carried extravagant hoops.

He nodded at the piano. "So Bruce was composing again," he said.

"He was putting some poetry of his sister's to music, for some kind of little theater deal she has in preparation, over in the City."

"How was he doing? I can't read music."

"Listen." She sat down at the piano. "I'm a lousy player myself, but this will give you the idea."

Darkness was smoking in through the walls. She had to peer close to see the notes; her hands stumbled on the keys. And yet she created something gentle for him. Afterward the sounds tinkled in his memory like rain in a young year.

She ended it with a destructive sweep of her knuckles across the board. As the jangled basses fell silent, she said roughly: "That's all. He never finished it."

"I wonder — " Kintyre remembered not to sit on the couch; he found a chair. "I wonder if the world may not have lost even more than you and I, Marge."

"I don't give a four-lettering damn about the world," she told him. She crossed the room and snapped the light switch. The sudden radiance was harsh to them, they both squinted. "I'd settle for having Bruce back."

"So would I. Naturally." He accepted the drink she offered and took a long swallow. It was heavy on the whisky and light on the soda. "And yet he was a scholar of unusual gifts. He even (he, my student) changed my opinions about some aspects of Machiavelli's thought — emphasized the idealism — he would, of course. I remember him quoting at me, '... *the best fortress is to be found in the love of the people.*' Isn't that exactly the sort of thing which would stick in Bruce's mind?"

"'The best fortress.'" She stared into her glass. "It didn't help him much, did it?"

Kintyre groped for another cigarette. He was smoking too much, he thought; he'd have a tongue like a fried shoe sole tomorrow.

"How much do you know?" he asked.

"Only a little." The eyes she raised to him from the couch were desperate. "Bob, what happened? Who did it to him?"

"I can't imagine," he said tonelessly.

"But — could it have been an accident, Bob? Maybe by mistake for someone else — could it have been?"

"Perhaps." *I lie in my flapping front teeth. You don't use pliers on a man without getting his name straight.*

"What was in the paper?" he asked. "I haven't seen."

"I don't know. I've been sitting here, ever since the policemen came. They asked me if I could guess — God!" She emptied her glass in three gulps.

"Could you?" he murmured. "I find it hard to conceive of anyone who might hate Bruce."

"There was Gene Michaelis," she said. "I've been thinking and thinking about him. He and his father. I met them once."

"Yes. I'd forgotten that. But Michaelis is a cripple now, remember? He couldn't — "

"Bruce was called over to San Francisco. Someone called him on the phone. Don't forget that. I can't forget it. I sat here while he talked! He didn't say what it was about, he just left. Took the train. He seemed excited, happy. Said he'd be out late and — " Margery's breath snapped into her lungs. "Bob! Gene Michaelis, sitting there and waiting for Bruce to come in — and those great ugly hands of his!"

Kintyre got up and went over to the couch. He sat down on its arm, next to her. She felt blindly for his fingers; her own were cold.

"The police think Bruce was killed by professional criminals," he said. "Can you imagine any reason why?"

"No." Her head shook. "No. Only Gene Michaelis — he swore that accident was Bruce's fault. He almost had Bruce thinking so. You didn't see Bruce then. You didn't see how he was affected by it, his old friend biting at him like a dog, accusing him and his sister of — " She gave Kintyre a blurred look. "That was how Bruce and I started to live together. There was nothing else that would help him. He'd already proposed to me. I didn't want to get married again — to him — to get married. And he'd had no thought in his silly head of being anything but a gentleman. Sure. I practically shanghaied him into bed with me. What else would get that thing off his mind, Gene Michaelis lying on the highway with both legs mashed? Gene was the only person who ever hated Bruce, and just being hated nearly destroyed him. He couldn't have made any other enemies — knowingly — he wasn't able to!"

That's not quite true, thought Kintyre briefly. *Jabez Owens.*

Margery's voice had risen raggedly, and her nails bit his palm. He stood up, pulling her after him by the wrist, and said: "Come on. We're getting out of here."

"What?" She blinked at him, as if waking from sleep.

"You're tired and scared and lonesome and hungry, and none of it is good. We're going out to dinner, and we'll talk about Bruce or whatever else you want, but we're going out."

"I have to work tomorrow," she protested.

"Cannonballs! Tell 'em you're down with Twonk's Disease and need the rest of the week off. Now grab your purse."

She followed him then, shivering. He drove her car slowly, to give her and the drink within her time; he spoke of trivia.

She hung back a moment when he had parked outside one of Oakland's first-class restaurants. "You can't afford this, Bob," she said.

"If you mention money once again, I'm going to wash your mouth out with five-dollar bills," he snapped. "Old greasy ones."

She smiled. "You know," she said, "you aren't so unlike Bruce after all. I remember how he also used to go out of his way for people. And then once when I tried to praise him for it, he answered, 'Ah, I'm no God damned saint.'"

"Sounds like Bruce," agreed Kintyre.

"He worshiped you," she said over the cocktails. "Did you know how much? You were everything he could dream of being, a traveler, an athlete, a scholar. He was even thinking of doing his military service in the Navy, because that's where you were. And then you treated him as an equal! You did more to make him happy than anyone else."

"I'd say you did," he parried, embarrassed.

"You know you pushed that affair." She was a little drunk, he saw, but no harm in that: under better circumstances, he'd have called it a happy drunk. "Remember how he and I first met? You were pub crawling with him one evening last year after you got back from Europe. You ran into me at the mulled-wine place; I was eating piroshki and looked very unglamorous, but I thought I'd have some fun with you — oh, hell, Bob, I thought there might be a chance to make you jealous — so I gave Bruce a big play. And you were delighted!"

"I thought he needed a girl friend," he said. "There's more in life than books and beer."

"You pander," she chuckled. "I'll bet you gloated when you found we were living in sin."

He shrugged. "If you can call it sin. Actually, Bruce was a very domestic type. I hoped you'd marry him."

"Sure," she said. "So I'm a very domestic type too, aren't I — ain't I — Bob, I know you don't like to dance, and your dancing is awful, but shall we try it just once before dinner?"

Afterward, when brandy and coffee were completing the meal, she said: "I'm still not sure if I was in love with Bruce or not. I always liked him. I think I was beginning to love him."

"I should imagine it would be hard not to, under the circumstances."

"He was the first man I ever knew who was — (a) — " she ticked the points off on her fingers — "interesting; which the solid citizens back in Ohio were not, not to me anyway — (b) reliable, which the local Bohemians are not."

"Please! Call me what else you will, but not a Berkeley Bohemian."

"You don't count. You're in a classification all by yourself. 'Reliable' was the wrong word. What do I mean? Faithful; steady; loving. I guess that's it. Loving — not himself, like most of these perpetual undergraduates; not — whatever you love, Bob, there must be something but I've never found out what unless it's that sailboat of yours. Bruce was loving of me. Loving all the world, but including me."

"You could call him tender," agreed Kintyre. "And yet he was a man. We took some rough hikes and pack trips, during the years we knew each other; and lately, after I got him interested in judo, he was doing very well. In the course of these amusements I've seen him get damaged now and then, sometimes rather badly. But he never admitted feeling any pain."

"I guess you'd consider that a virtue," she said.

They parked in the hills, with the Eastbay cities like a galaxy of stars below them, San Francisco an island universe across darkness. She sighed and leaned against him. He wondered, dimly alarmed, why he had come here.

"What are you going to do?" she asked him.

"Me? In the next few days, you mean? Oh, wind up his University work. Call on his family; haven't seen them in a long time now. What about you?"

"Carry on. What else is there?"

"I don't know," he said in his helplessness.

She turned to him and her fingers clawed at his coat. "Bob, don't take me back to my place," she whispered. "Not tonight. Don't leave me alone."

"Huh? But — "

"I know, I know, you're afraid I'll trap you — you conceited baboon. For Christ's sake, let me sleep on your floor tonight, I won't touch a hair of your sanctimonious head, but don't leave me alone!"

For the first time since he came to her, she began to cry.

The telephone woke him. He turned over, not wholly oriented. There was a woman sleeping beside him, wearing a pair of his pajamas. Where had he picked her up? Wait. Margery!

She slept very much like a child, curled in a ball. The pale foggy morning light touched a line of dried tears on her cheek. Kintyre remembered how she had clung to him. Nothing else had happened; she might have been his terrified young — No! That was a thought he clamped off before it had formed. Let it be said only that he had been a friend to her last night, and no more.

He was already padding into the kitchen, to pick up the phone before it woke her. "Hello," he said.

"Dr. Kintyre? Moffat."

"Oh — oh, yes, the officer. What is it?"

"I wondered if you knew what's become of Miss Margery Towne. She isn't at home." The voice had a bland none-of-my-business-but-I-do-need-help overtone. Had he spotted her car outside the house?

"I might be able to locate her, if it's urgent," said Kintyre cautiously; for it was in truth none of Moffat's business. "What's the trouble?"

"Burglary."

"What?"

"A neighbor heard noises in her place last night. Stewed about it for several hours, got no answer to the doorbell, finally called us. Our man had to go up the fire escape and in a broken window. The thief's route. It's a mess in there."

"The devil you say!"

"The devil it might be, sir. There were valuables, jewelry and so on, lying in plain sight. They don't seem to've been touched. I suppose the burglar was looking for something else. Have you any idea what it might have been?"

3

Kintyre returned home about noon. Gerald Clayton caught him on the phone with an invitation to lunch. Kintyre accepted readily. He had his share of false pride, but not so much that he wouldn't let a millionaire pick up the tab for a good meal.

The Fairhill Hotel sat in a swank area on the knees of the summer-brown hills walling the Eastbay. Kintyre parked his hand-me-down among mammaried Cadillacs and rump-sprung Plymouths and strolled into the lobby.

Clayton rose from a chair. "Ah, there, Bob, how are you?" He shook hands and moved toward the elevator. "Thought I'd have lunch sent up. But if you'd like a drink beforehand — "

"No, thanks. Maybe a bottle of beer with the meal. Uh, what's the occasion of all this?"

"We've things to talk about. Not too urgent, I guess, but I'm going to be tied up over in the City." Clayton took Kintyre's arm. "Anyhow, I felt like having some company for lunch."

He was fifty, still broad in the chest and erect in the spine, though his custom-made suit worked hard to disguise a beginning paunch. His grizzled auburn hair, brushed straight back, covered a long narrow head; nose and chin jutted out of a creased sinewy face which must once have been rather handsome. His eyes were deeply set, a darting dragonfly blue, without any burden of glasses. Kintyre liked him in a way, and felt sorry for him in a way, and sometimes wondered what the man was really thinking about.

"I heard about young Lombardi," said Clayton in the elevator. "It's a terrible thing."

"The police been after you too?" Kintyre's manner was abrupt; he didn't feel like more emotional scenes.

"I had one interview. They weren't interested in my alibi at all. What a disappointment: I had such a beautiful one. Witnesses to every waking hour. I came to Berkeley about noon Saturday, had a long conference with the manager of a local motorcycle agency, and a theater party which lasted late. Sunday I was at church, then I played golf, in the evening you were over for drinks, and Monday I went back to the City and spent all day in the office."

The elevator stopped and they got out and went down a long corridor. A little puzzled and annoyed, Kintyre said: "You protest too much."

Clayton opened his door. "I'm sorry," he answered. "I was trying to lighten my own mood, and it came out sounding as if I were trying to be funny. Bruce was a good kid."

He called room service. Kintyre's gaze strayed idly around the suite. Actually, Clayton's Bay Area interests centered in San Francisco. For the past several months he had kept an apartment there, while he went through the preliminary maneuvers of establishing a local branch of his import house. But the Eastbay was enough of a market in itself to justify Clayton in frequently staying at the Fairhill for days on end.

Though his latest checking in had been on Thursday, the suite bore little trace of him. His San Francisco rooms were just as impersonal; Kintyre doubted that the New York penthouse or the luxurious flat in Rome had been given more of a soul. There were four pictures, which apparently went wherever Clayton did: a thin blonde woman, with a washed-out kind of prettiness, who had been his first wife; and two young men and a girl, the children she had given him. Otherwise, nothing but business mail and business documents could be seen.

Oh, yes, Clayton smoked expensive cigars, and he had developed enough patter to get by in social circles whose small talk included the opera or Sartre's latest pronunciamento. But he had left no books lying around, only a news magazine; no chess set or cards or half-completed crossword puzzle; no private correspondence — well, if a man wanted to be simply a cash register, it was his privilege.

But Clayton wasn't that either, thought Kintyre. Something of the brash young salesman (where was it he started, Indianapolis? Some such place) and the construction-gang foreman of worsening days and the minor executive in a Midwestern wholesale house — something of what Margery would label "Babbitt," with all of her own class's glibness in labeling — remained in the transoceanic entrepreneur. Yes. But something else must have developed too. Kintyre had never quite discovered what. It was one reason he accepted most of Clayton's invitations.

"Okay, lunch will be on its way. Siddown, Bob."

Kintyre crossed his legs by the window and took out a cigarette. Clayton chose a cigar. "Do the police have a lead on Bruce's murder?" he asked.

"How should I know?"

"You were his best friend." Clayton's eyes locked with Kintyre's and held steady. "The boy wasn't killed for fun. Somehow, he asked for it. If we knew what he was doing in, say, the last week of his life —"

"Hm. You have a point. He was seeing a good deal of you also, wasn't he?"

"Yes. That's the main reason I asked you over today, Bob. Perhaps between us we could reconstruct most of his movements." Clayton chuckled. "Not that I think we'd solve the crime ourselves or any such nonsense, but organized information might help the police."

"Well — " Kintyre's memory walked backward into darkness. "Let me think....We were pretty busy till last week, with term's end and the start of final exams. After that it gets irregular, if you're on a faculty. You might have two exams on one day, and then none for three days. So Bruce had a certain amount of leisure all week. Huh — a week ago last Sunday — didn't he mention something about having gone across the Bay to see you?"

"He did." Clayton looked at a note pad. "He came up to my apartment to ask if I couldn't fix his older brother up with a job."

"So?"

"So I know that type. I'd met him, once before. I said no. Bruce got mad when I wouldn't even interview this Guido character."

Kintyre smiled. "I know what you mean. It's a side of him that not many people saw. He seldom lost his temper, but when it happened, it was awesome. I hope you kept yours."

"It wasn't easy," said Clayton. "Actually, this was not the first time we'd talked about the brother. There was once, some months ago — but I don't recall the details."

"I believe I remember. It came up à propos des bottes in my office, when you and he and I were discussing the Book of Witches, didn't it? He mentioned having this brother who spoke Italian. You doubted Guido would be qualified for any very responsible position. Yes, it comes back to me now, you got almost obnoxiously smug about how you had started from zero and so could anyone else."

"Less than zero in my case," said Clayton. His mouth twitched downward, ever so faintly.

"It riled Bruce," said Kintyre. "But he got over his mad fast enough. He was almost too reasonable for his own good."

"That sounds contradictory. I shouldn't think a really reasonable man would ever get angry."

"I beg to differ. Some things, it's unreasonable not to get furious about. Atrocities, including some governments whose existence is an atrocity. Or getting back to Bruce, there was the Point Perro incident several months ago."

"What was that?"

"Oh, nothing very important, I suppose. Point Perro is about sixty miles south on the coast highway. Uninhabited, though it's on any good map. Just a headland with a beach below, private property, fenced off, but I happen to know the owner and have his permission to use it. As isolated a spot, as primeval, as you'll find outside the High Sierras. Bruce and I took our sleeping bags down there for a weekend of surf casting. It has a deep-dropoff where the fish are apt to congregate at high tide. We found somebody had been dynamiting them, which had not only wasted and slaughtered fish but ruined some of the rock formations. Bruce followed the tire tracks above the cliffs, saw that the dynamiters had headed south, and insisted on following; He was quite ready to beat up on them himself. All we actually accomplished was to roust out the authorities, which spoiled our whole Saturday; but it never occurred to him to do less."

Kintyre sighed. "I suspect that he crusaded himself to his death, in just that manner."

"Let's return to our timetable," suggested Clayton. "Bruce stormed out of my place that Sunday night, but he did agree to come back the next afternoon. I said I'd think it over meanwhile, and he could bring Guido to see me after all."

"What happened?"

"They came together. I saw right off Guido was hopeless. Quite an amusing guy and all that, but once a bum always a bum. However, I made polite noncommittal noises. Hell, maybe I'll open a night club someday, and Guido can sing in it. That would be okay." Clayton drew on his cigar. "I didn't see Bruce again till that little party here Thursday night. Can you fill in the meantime?"

"Mmm — I had it all sorted out in my mind — yes. The Monday you speak of, I introduced Jabez Owens to Bruce. We all talked for about an hour in my office. Otherwise I think he just had a routine day, till he went over to your apartment."

"Tuesday?"

"More routine, except that Owens showed up as agreed and lent him the Borgia letters. Bruce took them home that night to look over."

"Oh, yes, those two were having quite an argument about it at the party. What's the deal, anyway? I didn't quite follow. Talking to Professor Ashwin most of the time, myself."

"Well, you know Owens is a writer, specializing in historical nonfiction on the popular level."

"I've heard the name, is all."

Kintyre drew the long breath of an experienced lecturer.

"Owens was a best seller in the late 1930's," he said. "Since the last official war, though, his sales have slipped. A couple of years back, he recouped with a thing called *Magnificent Monster: The Life and Times of Cesare Borgia*. Its scholarship is superficial — to put it kindly — but he has a flamboyant style and he dished up the sex and sadism with a liberal hand. All the old libels on Lucrezia are there, and so on. But it was a sensational seller even in hardback; the presses had trouble meeting the demand for pocket editions; and now Hollywood wants to film it as one of their more expensive superepics."

"So?" Clayton looked bored. "Good for him, but what has all this to do with Bruce?"

"Give me time. Prior to writing the book, Owens spent some months in Italy, allegedly doing research. He came back with certain letters he claims to have tracked down in the archives of a noble family — letters to and from Cesare, linking him with a cult of Satanists and all sorts of picturesque orgies and abominations.

"The correspondence stirred up a bit of professional controversy. If forged, it's skillfully done, and the noble family in question has been well bribed and well rehearsed. I suspect that is the case, myself. However, Owens has not unnaturally used the chance, not just to brag himself up as a scholarly detective, as if he'd found another cache of Boswell papers — he makes it pivotal to his whole book."

"Ah, yes. And now my Book of Witches manuscript —"

"Disproves it. The Book of Witches is unquestionably genuine, and certain statements in it pretty well clinch matters. *La vecchia religione* had been rooted out of the Romagna, even out of Liguria, long before Cesare Borgia was as much as a gleam in his daddy's apostolic eye. Therefore Owens' letters must be spurious. Either Owens had them cooked, or Owens was taken for a sucker himself.

"When he established this, some time back, Bruce wrote to the man. That was Bruce, of course. Give the poor chap a chance to back out gracefully, before publishing the evidence that will smear him over the landscape. Owens replied politely enough, asking for personal discussions. And so he arrived Sunday a week ago, en route to Hollywood from New York, and here he's been ever since."

"I shouldn't think he could keep the producer waiting like that," said Clayton.

"He has no firm commitment yet: only an invitation to come out and talk things over. A Piltdown-type scandal might cause the studio to back off. After all, if they want to do a life of Borgia, it's in the public domain. They don't have to pay Owens a nickel — unless, of course, they use the witch-cult material, in which case they'll doubtless pay him a fat sum and engage him as technical adviser to boot."

"Uh-huh." Clayton's eyes paled with thought.

"I keep getting sidetracked," complained Kintyre. "Also hoarse. I do want that beer now."

"In a minute, Bob. Let's continue this session first. You say Bruce took these letters home Tuesday night."

"Yes. I gathered he saw Owens again on Wednesday and returned them with the remark that he saw no reason to change his mind. There must have been quite an argument. I was at the dojo that evening, didn't see him till Thursday night, as a matter of fact. Then, of course, you had him and me and some of our colleagues — and Owens — up here for that stag party."

"I collect scholars," grinned Clayton.

Kintyre wondered if it might not literally be true. In the upper levels of the European business world, where Clayton spent half his time, a man was not respected for his money alone; he would get further if he could show some solid intellectual achievement. Clayton was hardly a social climber, but he must know the practical value of such kudos.

Any rich oaf of an American could buy paintings. Clayton was a bit more imaginative: he took up incunabula. And he invited specialists in, gave them liquor and sandwiches, turned them loose on each other, and sat around picking up the lingo.

And what's wrong with that? thought Kintyre. *Any Renaissance dignitary patronized artists and scholars in much the same way, for much the same reasons. So the Renaissance had its Leonardo, Rafael, Michelangelo — We throw our creative people out into the market place to peddle themselves to the general public. What do we have? Rock 'n' Roll.*

He jerked back to awareness. The other man was speaking: " — chemical tests. Owens said he wasn't going to let priceless relics be destroyed. It sounded phony to me."

"That was a real dogfight those two had." Kintyre shook his head admiringly.

"Never mind that now. Have you any information on Bruce's later movements?"

"Why, Friday he and I were both working hard. Saturday too he must have been. Yes, Friday afternoon was the last time I saw Bruce alive. We only said hello in passing. Margery Towne tells me he was home that evening and Saturday afternoon, otherwise apparently at the University."

"And that's all we can find out?" Clayton grimaced. "Not a hell of a lot, is it? Unless Miss Towne can tell — "

"One more thing," said Kintyre. "It may not be relevant. But her apartment was burgled last night."

The cigar dropped from Clayton's mouth. He bent over to pick it up, jerkily. His movements smoothed as Kintyre watched; when he raised himself and ground out the butt, his craggy face was under control.

"Surprised?" murmured Kintyre.

"Yes. Of course. What happened? What was taken?"

"That's the odd part. Nothing she knew of. Someone had broken in and made a hooraw's nest; but he, she, or it hadn't taken any silverware or jewelry, nothing."

"Uh." Clayton looked at his hands, folded in his lap, then back again, sharply. "How about papers?"

"We thought of that. The desks and drawers had been rooted through, all right, but nothing seemed to be missing."

"Would she know all about Bruce's papers?" Clayton fired the query like a policeman. "Don't stall, you damned Edwardian. I know she was his mistress."

"I don't happen to like that word in that particular connection," said Kintyre gently. "However — she hadn't seen all of Bruce's letters and notes. He kept them in a couple of cardboard filing boxes. They didn't seem even to have been opened, though."

"Did you look in to make sure?"

"No. Should we have?"

"I guess not." Clayton rubbed his chin. "No, I wouldn't bother. Because the burglar was evidently looking for something he thought might be in the apartment, but which wasn't. Something that might be in a desk or a bureau drawer, but was too large to fit into a filing box or a — any such thing."

"As what?" challenged Kintyre.

He had already guessed the answer: "The Book of Witches is a fairly big volume."

Kintyre nodded. He was on the point of repeating what Margery had said to him, when they stood in the ruins after the police had gone.

She poured herself a drink with shaking hands. A sunbeam splashed pale copper in her still tousled hair. She said: "That bastard. That crawling bastard. Why didn't I tell the cops?"

"Who?"

"Owens, of course! Who d'you think would come sneaking in here? What might we have of any use to anybody, except that old book Bruce was studying — the one that could torpedo Owens and his big movie sale and his precious reputation. Owens came in here to try and find that book and take it and burn it!"

She tossed off her drink neat, poured another and glared at Kintyre. "Well?" she snarled.

"Well, it's a serious accusation to make," he replied.

"Serious my left buttock! You know what that snake already tried to do? He tried to bribe Bruce! Bruce told me about it. Friday after that stag party, Owens came to his office and talked all around the subject and — oh, he was pious-sounding enough about it, he knows his euphemisms. But he offered Bruce five thousand dollars to suppress his findings about witches in Italy. Five thousand bucks — Christ, the movies can pay him a quarter of a million!"

"I take it, then, you're insulted by the size of the bribe."

The attempt to jolly her didn't come off. She said viciously: "Bruce boiled over. He was still boiling when he came home. He told Owens to his face, he'd write an article about his research the minute he returned from your pack trip — he'd inform the newspapers, so the whole public could know the truth — Bob!"

It was a scream in her throat.

"What is it?" he cried, turning toward her in alarm.

"Bob — do you think.... Oh, no, Bob!"

"What's the matter?" asked Clayton.

Kintyre shook himself. "Nothing. The manuscript is still with us, naturally," he said in a flat voice. "Bruce kept it in his office. I stopped by today and locked it in a safe."

"Owens —"

"Look here," said Kintyre angrily, "I went through this once before, with Miss Towne. I don't hold with talebearing. The police are competent, and have the essential facts already. Unless more evidence turns up to change my mind, I see no reason to run to them with any sordid little story of academic intrigue which can't even be proved."

However, his brain continued, *while I'm in no position to pay fees, Trig isn't very busy these days. He may enjoy looking into the recent movements of a murder suspect.*

There was a knock on the door and a bellboy wheeled in lunch.

4

Not until evening was Kintyre free to cross the bridge into San Francisco. He had spent hours on Bruce's uncorrected papers, and talked with Yamamura, who said he would sniff around, and he had called Margery on the phone to see if she was all right.

"Come over and take potluck, Bob," she said. He sensed loneliness. But — hell's boiling pots, she made him feel cluttered!

"I'm afraid I can't," he evaded. "Commitments. But take it easy, huh? Go visit someone, go have a cup of espresso, don't sit home and nest on your troubles. I'll see you soon."

He poured himself a small drink after hanging up and tossed it off. Then he changed into his darkest suit and got the car rolling. Personally, he would not have placarded a loss on his clothes, but Bruce's parents were from the Old World.

As he hummed along the freeway and over the great double span of the bridge (Bruce must have been carried dead in the opposite direction, wedged in a corner so the tollgate guard would think him merely asleep; doubtless the police were checking the memories of all night shift men) Kintyre rehearsed the career of the Lombardis. Bruce was the only one he had really known, though he had been over there for dinner a few times. The parents had been very respectful, innocently happy that their son should be friends with a Doctor of Philosophy. His mother made good pasta....

There wasn't much to remember. Angelo Lombardi was a Genoese sailor. Chronic hard times were not improved when his son Guido came along. Nor did he see much of his young wife. (Did Maria's years of being mostly alone in a dingy tenement, with nobody to love but one little boy, account for what Guido had become?) In 1930 the family arrived as immigrants at San Francisco. Here Angelo worked in the commercial fishing fleet; here Bruce and the daughter were born; here he saved enough money to buy his own boat; here he lost it again in a collision — by God, yes, it had been a collision with Peter Michaelis' single craft. Feeling the years upon him, Angelo used the insurance money to start a restaurant. It had neither failed nor greatly prospered: it gave him a living and little more.

Yet Angelo Lombardi had remained a man with hope.

Kintyre turned off at the first ramp, twisted through the downtown area, and got onto Columbus Avenue and so to North Beach. Hm, let's see — a minor street near the Chinatown fringe — uh-huh.

The sky was just turning purple when he stopped in front of the place: Genoa Café set in a two-story frame building perpetrated, with bays and turrets, right after the 1906 fire. It was flanked by a Chinese grocery store, full of leathery fragrances, and a Portuguese Baptist mission. A sign on the door said closed. Well, the old people would be in no mood for discussing the various types of pizza tonight.

Yellow light spilled from the upper windows. Kintyre found the door to the upstairs apartment and rang the bell.

A street lamp blinked to life, a car went by, a grimy urchin watched him impassively from a doorway across the road. He felt much alone.

He heard feet coming down the stairs, a woman's light quick tread. Expecting Maria Lombardi, he took off his hat and bowed in Continental style when the door opened. He stopped halfway through the gesture and remained staring.

Morna, he thought, and he stood on the schooner's deck as it heeled to the wind, and she was grasping the mainmast shrouds with one hand, crouched on the rail and shading her eyes across an ocean that glittered. Her yellow hair blew back into his face, it smelled of summer.

"Yes?"

Kintyre shook himself, like a dog come out of a deep hurried river. "I'm sorry," he stammered. "I'm sorry. You startled me, looked like someone I used to — " He pulled the chilly twilight air into his lungs, until he could almost feel them stretch. One by one, his muscles relaxed.

"Miss Lombardi, isn't it?" he tried again. "I haven't seen you for a couple of years, and you wore your hair differently then. I'm Robert Kintyre."

"Oh, yes. I remember you well," she said. Her mouth turned a little upward, its tautness gentling. "Bruce's professor. He spoke of you so often. It's very kind of you to come."

She stood aside to let him precede her. His hand brushed hers accidentally in the narrow entrance. Halfway up the stairs, he realized he was holding the fist clenched.

What is this farce? he asked himself angrily. Nothing more than straight blonde hair, worn in bangs across the forehead and falling to the shoulders. Now in the full electric light he could see that it wasn't even the same hue, a good deal darker than Morna's weather-bleached mane. And Corinna Lombardi was a mature woman — young, he recalled Bruce's going over to the City last month for her twenty-second birthday party — but grown. Morna would always be thirteen.

Corinna had been nineteen when he saw her last, still living here and working in the café. That was at a little farewell dinner the Lombardis had given him, before he departed for his latest year in Italy. They had wanted him to look up Angelo's brother Luigi, the one who had made a success in the old country as a secret service man. Kintyre had visited Luigi a few times, finding him a pleasant sort with scholarly inclinations, most interested in his brilliant nephew Bruce, with whom he corresponded.

At any rate, Kintyre had had too much else to think about to pay much attention to a quiet girl. By the time he returned, as Bruce told him, she had left home after a spectacular quarrel with her parents. That was soon repaired — it had only been a declaration of independence — but she had kept her own job and her own apartment since then.

The rambling of his mind soothed him. At the time he did not realize that, down underneath, his mind was telling itself about Corinna Lombardi. It decided that she had few elements of conventional prettiness. She was tall, and her figure was good except that the shoulders were too wide and the bust too small for this decade's canons. Her face was broad, with high cheek-bones and square jaw and straight strong nose; it had seen a good deal of sun. Her eyes were greenish-gray under heavy dark brows, her mouth was wide and full, her voice was low. She wore a black dress, as expected, and a defiant bronze pin in the shape of a weasel.

Then Kintyre had emerged on the landing, and Angelo Lombardi — thickset, heavy-faced, balding — engulfed his hand in an enormous sailor's paw. "Come in, sir, please to come in and have a small glass with us."

Maria Lombardi rose for the Doctor of Philosophy. Her light-brown hair and clear profile told whence her children had their looks; he suspected that much of the brains had come from her too. "How do you do, Professor Keen-teer. We thank you for coming."

He sat down, awkwardly. Overstuffed and ghastly, the living room belonged to a million immigrants of the last generation, who had built from empty pockets up to the middle class. But families like this would eat beans oftener than necessary for twenty years, so they could save enough to put one child through college. Bruce had been the one.

"I just came to express my sympathy," said Kintyre. He felt himself under the cool green appraisal of Corinna's eyes, but could not think of words less banal. "Can I do anything to help? Anything at all?"

"You are very kind," said old Lombardi. He poured from what was evidently his best bottle of wine. "Everyone has been so kind."

"Do you know what his room was like, the past half of a year, Professor?" asked Maria. "He never invited us there."

I rather imagine not, thought Kintyre wryly. "Nothing unusual," he said. "I'll bring you his personal effects as soon as I can."

"Professor," said Lombardi. He leaned his bulk forward very slowly. The glass shivered in his fingers. "You knew my son so well. What do you think happen to him?"

"I only know what the police told me," said Kintyre.

Maria crossed herself. She closed her eyes, and he did not watch her moving lips; that conversation didn't concern him.

"My son he was murdered," said Lombardi in an uncomprehending voice. "Why did they murder him?"

"I don't know," insisted Kintyre. "The police will find out."

Corinna left her chair and came around to stand before the men. It was a long stride, made longer by wrath. She put her hands on her hips and said coldly:

"Dr. Kintyre, you're not naïve. You must know murder is one of the safest crimes there is to commit. What's the actual probability that they'll ever learn who did it, when they claim they haven't even a motive to guide them?"

Kintyre couldn't help bristling a trifle. She was tired and filled with grief, but he had done nothing to rate such a tone. He clipped off his words: "If you think you have a clue, Miss Lombardi, you should take it to the authorities, not to me."

"I did," she said harshly. "They were polite to the hysterical female. They'll look into it, sure. And when they see he has an alibi — as he will! — they won't look any further."

Maria stood up. "Corinna!" she exclaimed. "*Basta, figliolaccia!*"

The girl wrenched free of her mother's hand. "Oh, yes," she said, "that's how it was with the policeman too. With everybody. Don't pick on the poor cripple. Haven't you been enough of a jinx to him? Don't you see, that's exactly what he thinks! That's why he killed Bruce!"

An inner door opened, and a man entered the room. He was thirty years old, with a strong burly frame turning a little fat. He was good-looking in a dark heavy-lipped way, his hair black and curly, his eyes a restless rusty brown, nose snubbed and jaw underslung. He wore tight black trousers with a silver stripe, a cummerbund, a white silk shirt open halfway down his chest; he carried a cased guitar under one arm.

"Oh," he said. "I thought somebody'd come. Hello, Doc."

"Hello, Guido," said Kintyre, not getting up. He had nothing personally against Bruce's older brother, who had been quite a charming devil the few casual times they met. However — "*He who does not choose the path of good, chooses to take the path of evil,*" said Machiavelli's *Discourses*: and Guido had been an anchor around more necks than one.

"Don't get in a bind, kitten," he said to his sister. "I could hear you making with the grand opera a mile upwind."

She whirled about on him, shaking, and said: "You could let him get cold before you went back to that club to sing your dirty little songs."

"My girl, you speak the purest B.S., as Bruce would have been the first to tell you." Guido smiled, took out a cigarette one-handed and stuck it in his mouth. "I was out of town the whole weekend, just when the cats go real crazy. If I don't make with it tonight, the man will ignite me, and what good would that do Bruce?" He flipped out a book of matches, opened it and struck one, all with the same expert hand.

Corinna's gaze went from face to face, and a beaten look crept into it. "Nobody cares," she whispered. "Just nobody cares."

She sat down. Lombardi twisted his fingers, looking wretched; Maria folded herself stiffly into a chair; Guido leaned on the doorjamb and blew smoke.

Kintyre felt, obscurely, that it depended on him to ease the girl. He said: "Please, Miss Lombardi. We don't mean that. But what can we do? We'd only get in the way of the police."

"I know, I know." She got it out between her teeth, while she looked at the floor. "Let George do it. Isn't that the motto of this whole civilization? Someday George isn't going to be around to do it, and we'll have gotten too flabby to help ourselves."

It paralleled some of his own thinking so closely that he was startled. But he said, "Well, you can't declare a vendetta, can you?"

"Oh, be quiet!" She looked up at him with a smoldering under her brows. "Of course I don't mean that. But I know who must have done it, and I know he'll have some kind of story, and no one will look past that story, because he seems like such a pathetic case. And he isn't! I know Gene and Peter Michaelis. They got what was coming to them!"

"Too much!" roared Lombardi. "Now you be still!" She ignored him. Her eyes would not release Kintyre's.

"Well?" she said after a moment.

He wondered if it was only her misery which clawed at him, or if she was always such a harpy. He said with great care: "Well, in theory any of us could be guilty. I might have done it because Bruce was — going around with a girl I used to know. Or Guido here — jealousy? A quarrel? I assume we have merely his word he was out of town on Saturday and Sunday. Shall we also ask the police to check every minute of his weekend?"

The man in the doorway flushed. "Dig that," he said slowly. "So you're going to — "

"Nothing of the sort," rapped Kintyre. "I was trying to show how a private suspicion is no grounds for — "

Guido took a long drag on his cigarette, snuffed it in a horrible souvenir ashtray, and left without a word. They heard his footfalls go down the stairs.

"I am *so* sorry, Mister Professor," faltered Lombardi.

"*Niente affatto, signor.*" Kintyre stood up. "All of you are worn out." He essayed a smile at Corinna. "You were echoing some of my own principles. We pessimists ought to stick together."

She did not even turn her face toward him. But her profile was one he could imagine on Nike of Samothrace, the Victory which strides in the wind.

"I've always thought principles should be acted on," she told him sullenly.

"Corinna!" said Maria. Her daughter paid no attention.

Kintyre took his leave in a confusion of apologies. When he stood alone on the dusky street, he whistled. That had been no fun.

But now it was over with. He could let things cool down for a week or so, then deliver Bruce's possessions, and say farewell with an insincere promise to "look you up soon, when I get the chance." And there would be an end of that.

But he had thought for a heartbeat she was Morna come home to him.

His fingers were wooden, hunting for a cigarette; he dropped the pack on the sidewalk before getting one out. He could feel the first onset of the horror, moving up along the channels of his brain.

Sometimes, he thought with a remnant of coolness, sometimes distraction could head off the trouble. If he could get involved in something outside himself, and yet important to himself, so that his whole attention was engaged, the horror might retreat.

He yanked smoke into his lungs, blew it forth, tossed the cigarette to the paving and stamped on it. Then he went into the grocery. There was a public phone on the wall, he leafed through the directory until he found the name.

Michaelis Peter C.

5

He didn't call ahead, but drove on down. When he parked and got out, he saw Coit Tower whitely lit above him, on the steep art-colony heights of Telegraph Hill. Not many blocks away was Fisherman's Wharf, a lot of tourist pits and a few authentic restaurants. But here he stood in a pocket of slum, before a rotting rattrap tenement. A single street lamp a block away cast a purulent light at its own foot. Elsewhere the night flowed. He heard the nearby rattle of a switch engine, pushing freight cars over iron; a battered cat slunk past him; otherwise he was alone.

He walked across to the house with forced briskness, struck a match and hunted through several grimy scrawls on mailboxes before Michaelis' name came to him. Number 8.

The main entrance was unlocked. The hall, dusty in threadbare carpeting, held dim electric bulbs. He heard noises through some of the doors, and smelled stale cooking. A glance told him Number 8 must be upstairs. He climbed, only now starting to wonder just how he planned to do his errand.

Or what his errand was, if it came to that.

Bruce had never spoken much to him of Gene Michaelis. They had been children together on the waterfront. Bruce was a year younger, doubtless a quiet bookish sort, teacher's pet, even then — but apparently unaffected by it, so that he was not disliked. Still, he must have been lonely. And Gene was a rough-and-tumble fisherman's son. Nevertheless, one of those odd fierce boy-friendships had existed between them. Bruce had probably dominated it, without either of them realizing the fact.

In time they drifted apart. Gene had left high school at sixteen, Bruce had said, after some whoopdedo involving a girl; he had tramped since then, dock walloper, fry cook, bouncer, sales-man — he found it easy to lie about his age. Now and then he revisited the Bay Area. His return from Navy service had been last summer, when Kintyre was still in Europe; Kintyre had never actually met him. Gene had looked up Bruce in Berkeley, and through Bruce renewed an acquaintance with Corinna, and after that Gene had moved over to San Francisco.

Number 8. Kintyre heard television bray through the thin panels. He looked at his watch. Past ten o'clock. *Oh, hell, let's play by ear.* He knocked.

Feet shuffled inside. The door opened. Kintyre looked slightly upward, into a lined heavy face with a thick hook nose and small black eyes and a gray bristle of hair. The man had shoulders like a Mack truck, and there wasn't much of a belly on him yet. He wore faded work clothes. The smell of cheap wine was thick around him.

"What do you want?" he said.

"Mr. Michaelis? My name's Kintyre. I'd like to talk to you for a few minutes."

"We're not buying any, and if you're from the finance company you can — " Michaelis completed the suggestion.

"Neither," said Kintyre mildly. "Call me a sort of ambassador."

Puzzled, Michaelis stood aside. Kintyre walked into a one-room apartment with a curtained-off cooking area. A wall bed was opened out, unmade. There were a few chairs, a table with a half-empty gallon of red ink on it, a television set, a tobacco haze, much dust and many old newspapers on the floor.

Gene Michaelis occupied a decaying armchair. He was a young, black-haired version of his father, and would have been rather handsome if he smiled. He wore flannel pajamas which had not been washed for some time. His legs stuck rigidly out before him, ending in shoes whose heels rested on the floor. Two canes leaned within reach. He was smoking, drinking wine, and watching the screen; he did not stop when Kintyre entered.

"I'm sorry the place is such a mess," said Peter Michaelis. He spoke fast, with an alcoholic slur. "It's kind of hard. My wife's dead, and my son has to live with me and he can't do nothing. When I get home from looking for work, all day looking for a job, I'm too tired to clean up." He made vague dusting motions over a chair. "Siddown. Drink?"

"No, thanks." Kintyre lowered himself. "I came — "

"I was already down in the world when this happened last year," said Michaelis. "I owned my own boat once. Yes, I did. The *Ruthie M.* But then she got sunk, and there wasn't enough insurance to get another, and well, I ended up as a deckhand again. Me, who'd owned my own boat." He sat and blinked muzzily at his guest.

"I'm sorry to hear that. But — "

"Then my wife died. Then my son come back from the Navy, and got himself hurt real bad. Both legs gone, above the knees. It took all the money I had to pay the doctors. I quit work to take care of my son. He was in a bad way. When he got so he could look after himself a little, I went looking for my job back, only I didn't get it. And since then I haven't found nothing."

"Well," said Kintyre, "there's the welfare, and rehabilitation — "

Gene turned around and said a short obscenity.

"That's what they'll do for you," he added. "They found me a job basket weaving. *Basket weaving!* Kee-rist, I was a gunner's mate in the Navy. Basket weaving!"

"I'm a Navy man myself," ventured Kintyre. "Or was, after Pearl Harbor. Destroyers."

"What rank were you? A brown-nosing officer, I'll bet."

"Well — "

"A brass hat. Kee-rist." Gene Michaelis turned back to his television.

"I'm sorry," muttered his father. "It's not so easy for him, you know. He was as strong and lively a young fellow as you could hope to see. God, six months ago! Now what's he got to do all day?"

"I'm not offended," said Kintyre. *I would, in fact, be inclined to take offense only at a system of so-called education which has so little discipline left in it that its victims are unable to do more than watch this monkey show when the evil days have come. But that is not of immediate relevance.*

"What did you come for?" Peter Michaelis lifted his bull head and his voice crested: "You know of a job?" He sagged back again. "No. No, you wouldn't."

"I'm afraid not," said Kintyre. "I came as — I came to help you in another way." *Maledetto! How much like Norman Vincent Peale is one man allowed to sound? But I can't think of anything else.*

"Yes?" Michaelis sat erect; even Gene twisted half around.

"You know the Lombardi family, of course."

"Do we know them?" spat Michaelis. "I wish to hell we didn't!"

"Have you heard that the son, Bruce, is dead?"

"Uh-huh," said Gene. He turned down the sound of his program and added with a certain pleasure: "Looks like there's some justice in the world after all."

"Now, wait," began Kintyre.

Gene turned more fully to face the visitor. His eyes narrowed. "What have you got to do with them?" he asked.

"I knew Bruce. I thought — "

"Sure. You thought he was God's little bare-bottomed baby angel. I know. Everybody does. It took a long time to get down past all those layers of holy grease on him. I did."

"You know what the old man done to me?" shouted Peter Michaelis. "He rammed me. Sent my boat to the bottom in 1945. He murdered two of my crew. They drowned. I could of been drowned myself!"

Kintyre remembered Bruce's account. A freakish, sudden fog had been blown down a strong wind. Such impossibilities do happen now and then. The boats blundered together and sank. The Coast Guard inquiry found it an act of God; Michaelis tried to sue, but the case was thrown out of court. Then, for the sake of their sons, Peter and Angelo made a grudging peace.

What had happened lately must have brought all the old bitterness back, with a dozen years' interest added.

"Shut up," said Gene. He was drunk too, Kintyre saw, but cold drunk, in control of everything except his emotions. "Shut up, Pete. It was an accident. Why should he ruin his own business?"

"He got him a restaurant out of it," mumbled Michaelis. "What have we got?"

"Look here," said Kintyre, not very truthfully. "I'm a neutral party. I didn't have to come around here, and there's nothing in it for me. But will you listen?"

"If you'll listen too," said Gene. He poured himself another glass. "Huh. I know what the Lombardis been telling you about me. Let me tell you about them."

Somewhere in the back of Kintyre's mind, a thin little warning whistle blew. He grabbed the arms of his chair and hung on tight. There was no time now to add up reasons why; he knew only that if he let Gene talk freely about Corinna, there was going to be trouble.

"Never mind," he said coldly. "I'm not interested in that aspect. I came here because I don't think you murdered Bruce Lombardi and the police may think you did."

That stopped them. Peter Michaelis looked up, his face turning a drained color. Gene puckered his lips, snapped them together, and went blank of expression. His dark gaze did not waver from Kintyre's, and he said quite steadily: "What are you getting at?"

"Bruce was called over to the City by someone last Saturday evening," said Kintyre. "His body was found Monday morning. You know very well that if you'd called him, offering to patch up the quarrel, he'd have come like a shot. Where were you two this weekend?"

"Why — " Peter Michaelis' voice wobbled. "I was home all day Saturday — housework. Went out for a drink at night — church Sunday morning, yeah, then came back for a nap. Hey, I played pinochle down in front of the warehouse that evening with — " His words trailed off.

"Nobody glanced in, then?" asked Kintyre. "No one who could verify that Bruce wasn't lying bound and gagged?"

"Why — I — "

"Hey!" Gene Michaelis surged to his feet. It was a single swinging leap, propelled upward by his arms. His aluminum legs spraddled, seeking clumsily for a foothold. Somehow he got one of his canes and leaned on it.

"What business is it of yours, anyway?" he snarled.

Can I tell you that I don't know? thought Kintyre. *Can I tell you I'm here because a girl I'd scarcely seen before now wanted me to come?*

Hardly.

He leaned back with strained casualness and said: "I want to make peace between your two families. Call it a gesture toward Bruce. I admit I liked him. And he never stopped liking you, Gene.

"If you keep on spewing hatred at the Lombardis as you have been, the police are going to get very interested in your weekend. Where were you?"

Gene hunched his shoulders. "None of your God damn business."

"I take it you weren't home, then."

"No, I was not. If you want to ask any more, let's see your Junior G-man badge."

Kintyre sighed. "All right." He stood up. "I'll go. The cops won't be so obliging, if you don't cooperate with them."

He looked past Gene, to the window. It was a hole into total blackness. He wondered if that had been the last sight Bruce saw — of all this earth of majesty, a single smeared window opening on the dark.

"I didn't do it," said Gene. "We didn't." He showed his teeth. "But I say three cheers for whoever did. I'd like to get the lot of 'em here, that sister now — "

"Hold on!" The violence of his tone shivered Kintyre's skull. Afterward it was a wonder to him, how rage had leaped up.

Gene swayed for a moment. An unpleasant twisting went along his lips. Beside Kintyre, the father also rose, massive and watchful.

"So you'd like some of that too, would you?" said Gene. "You won't get it. She's only a whore inside. Outside, she's like a goddam nun. You know what we call that kind where I come from? Pri — "

"I'm going," said Kintyre harshly. "I prefer to be among men."

Unthinkingly, he had chosen the crudest cut. He saw that at once. A physical creature like Gene Michaelis, whose sexual exploits must have been his one wall against every hidden inadequacy, must now be feeling nearly unmanned.

Gene roared. His cane lifted and whistled down.

It could have been a head-smashing blow. Kintyre stepped from it and it jarred against the floor. The cane broke across. Gene rocked forward on his artificial legs, his hands reaching out for Kintyre's throat.

Kintyre planted himself passively, waiting. He didn't want to hit a cripple. Nor would fists be much use against all that bone and meat.

As Gene lunged, Kintyre slipped a few inches to one side, so the clutching arm went above his shoulder. He took it in his hands, his knee helped the great body along, and Gene Michaelis crashed into the wall.

As the cloud of plaster exploded, Kintyre saw the old man attack. Peter Michaelis was still as strong as a wild ox, and as wrathful.

Kintyre could have killed him with no trouble.

Kintyre had no wish to. Anyone could be driven berserk, given enough low-grade alcohol on top of enough wretchedness. He waited again, until the fisherman's fist came about in a round-house swing. There was time enough for a judo man to get out of the way, catch that arm, spin the opponent halfway around, and send him on his way. It would have been more scientific to throttle him unconscious, but that would have taken a few seconds and Gene was crawling back to his feet.

"Let's call it a day," said Kintyre. "I'm not after a fight."

"You — filthy — bastard." Gene tottered erect. Blood ran down one side of his mouth; the breath sobbed in and out of him; but he came.

On the way he picked up the other cane.

He tried to jab with it. Kintyre took it away from him. As simple as that — let the stick's own motion carry it out of the opponent's hand. Gene bellowed and fell. Kintyre rapped him lightly on the head, to discourage him.

Someone was pounding on the door. "What's going on in there? Hey, what's going on?"

"I recommend you cooperate with the police," said Kintyre. "Wherever you were this weekend, Gene, tell them. They'll find out eventually."

He opened the window, went through, and hung for a moment by his hands. Father and son were sitting up, not much damaged. Kintyre straightened his elbows and let go. It wasn't too long a drop to the street, if you knew how to land.

He went to his car and got in. There was no especial sense of victory within him: a growing dark feeling of his own momentum, perhaps. He had to keep moving, the horror was not yet asleep.

All right, Corinna, he thought as the motor whirred to life. It was a bit childish, but he was not in any normal state. *I did your job. Now I'll do one for myself.*

6

When Bruce last mentioned Guido to Kintyre, not so long ago, the name of the Alley Cat occurred. Presumably Guido was still singing there. Kintyre looked up the address in a drug-store phone book. It was back in North Beach, of course, in a subdistrict which proved to be quiet, shabby, and tough.

There was no neon sign to guide him, only a flight of stairs downward to a door with the name painted on it. Once past a solid-looking bouncer, he found a dark low-ceilinged room, decorated with abstract murals and a few mobiles. The bar was opposite him. Otherwise the walls were lined with booths, advantageously deep, and the floor was packed with tables. Most of the light came from candles on these, in old wax-crusted Chianti bottles. Patronage was thin this evening, perhaps a dozen couples and as many stags. They ran to type: either barely of drinking age or else quite gray, the men with their long hair and half-open blouses more ornate than most of the women, a few obvious faggots, a crop-headed girl in a man's shirt and trousers holding hands with a more female-looking one.

Hipsters, professionally futile; students, many of whom would never leave the warm walls of academe; a Communist or two, or a disillusioned ex-Communist who had not found a fresh illusion, perpetually refighting the Spanish Civil War; self-appointed intellectuals who had long ago stopped learning or forgetting; dabblers in art or religion or the dance; petty racketeers, some with a college degree but no will to make use of it — Kintyre stopped enumerating. He knew these people. One of his strictures on Margery was her weakness for such a crowd. They bored him.

Guido sat on a dais near the bar, draped around a high stool with a glass of beer handy. His fingers tickled the guitar strings, they responded with life, he bore his brother's musical gifts. His voice was better than Bruce's:

> " — *Who lived long years ago.*
> *He ruled the land with an iron hand*
> *But his mind was weak and low —* "

Despite himself, Kintyre was amused to find such an old acquaintance here. He wondered if Guido knew the author.

He threaded between the tables till he reached one close by the platform. Guido's glance touched him, and the curly head made a half-nod of recognition.

Since he would be overcharged anyway, Kintyre ordered an import beer and settled back to nurse it. The ballad went on to its indelicate conclusion. Guido ended with a crashing chord and finished his brew at a gulp. There was light applause and buzzing conversation.

Guido leaned back against the wall. His eyelids drooped and he drew wholly different sounds from the strings. Talk died away. Not many here would know this song. Kintyre himself didn't recognize it before the singer had embarked on the haunting refrain. Then Guido looked his way, smiling a little, and he knew it was a gift to him.

> "*Quant' è bella giovinezza*
> *Che si fugge tuttavia!*
> *Di doman' non c' è certezza:*
> *Chi vuol esse lieto, sia!*"

Lorenzo the Magnificent had written it, long ago in the days of pride.

When he finished, Guido said, "*Entr'acte*," laid down his guitar, and came over to Kintyre's table. He stood with his left hand on his hip, fetching out a cigarette and lighting it with the right.

"Thanks," said Kintyre.

Guido continued the business with the cigarette, taking his time. Kintyre returned to his beer.

"Well," said Guido finally. He grinned. "You're a cool one. I mean in every sense of the word. Let's find a booth."

They sat down on opposite sides of the recessed table. A handsome young waitress lit the candle for them. "On me," said Guido.

"Same, then," said Kintyre, emptying his glass.

Guido squirmed. "How d'you like the place?" he asked.

Kintyre shrugged. "It's a place."

"This Parisian bistro deal is only on slack nights. Weekends, we got a combo in here."

"I think I prefer the bistro."

"I guess you would."

They fell back into silence. Guido smoked raggedly. Kintyre felt no need for tobacco; the implacable sense of going somewhere overrode his self.

After the girl had brought their round, Guido said in a harsh tone, looking away from him: "Well, what is it? I got to go on again soon."

"I just came from the Michaelis'," said Kintyre.

"What?" Guido jerked. "What'd you go there for?"

"Let's say I was curious. Gene Michaelis was out of sight last weekend. He won't say where."

"You don't — " Guido looked up. Something congealed in him. "I thought Corinna was just flipping," he said, very softly.

"I don't accuse anyone," said Kintyre. "I'm only a civilian. However, the police are going to give him a rough time if he won't alibi himself."

Guido lit a fresh cigarette from the butt of the last.

"Where were you, Saturday afternoon through Monday morning?" Kintyre tossed the question off as lightly as he was able.

"Out of town," said Guido. "With some friends."

"You'd better get in touch with them, then, so they can give statements to that effect."

"They — Christ almighty!" In the guttering flamelight, Kintyre saw how sweat began to film the faun countenance.

"My personal opinion," he said, watching Guido's lips fight to stiffen themselves, "is that you are not involved. The fact remains, though, you'd better account for your weekend."

"To you?" It was a wan little truculence.

"I can't force you. But without trying to play detective, I am sticking my nose a ways into this affair. Knowing the people concerned, I might possibly turn up something the police can use.

"So where did you spend your weekend, Guido?"

The full mouth pouted. "Rotate, cat, rotate. Why should anybody care? Where's my motive?"

"Where is anyone's motive? You have a lot of shady friends. I daresay your mother had to shield you often enough from your father — or even from the authorities, once or twice." It was a guess on Kintyre's part, but he saw that he had struck a target. "Maybe of late you've gotten mixed up with something worse. Maybe Bruce found out."

"Beat feet," said Guido. "Blow before I call the bouncer."

"I'm merely trying to reason as a policeman might. I'm not accusing you, I'm warning you."

"Well," said Guido, raising his eyes again, "there wasn't anything like that going on. Certainly nothing Bruce would know about. I mean, man, he was all professor!"

"Jealousy," murmured Kintyre. "There's another motive. Bruce was the favorite. All his life he was the favorite. Oh, he deserved it — the well-behaved kid, the bright and promising kid. But it must have been hard for you to take, with your Italian background, where the oldest son normally has precedence. You were college material too. It just so happened Bruce was better, and there was only money for one. Of course, later you had your G.I., and didn't use it. You'd lost interest. Which doesn't change the fact: money was spent on Bruce that might otherwise have been spent on you."

Guido finished his whisky and signaled out the booth. "Crazy," he fleered. "But go on."

"Well, let's see. I imagine you're always at loggerheads with your father. That won't recommend you to a suspicious detective either. Here you are, thirty years old, and except for your military hitch you've always lived at home. You've sponged, between short-lived half-hearted jobs; you've drifted from one night club engagement to another, but all small time and steadily getting smaller. I hardly think you belong to the Church any more, do you?"

"I was kicked out," admitted Guido with a certain cockiness. "I got married a few years back. It didn't take. So I got divorced and the Church kicked me out. Not that I'd believed that guff for a long time before. But there was quite a row."

The waitress looked into the booth. Guido slid a hand down her hip. "Let's have a bottle in here," he said. "Raus!" He slapped her heartily on the rump. His gaze followed her toward the bar.

"Nice piece, that," he said. "Maybe I can fix you up with her, if you want."

"No, thanks," said Kintyre.

Guido was winning back his confidence. He grinned and said: "Sure. I'm the bad boy. Bruce worked part time all his undergraduate years, and made his own way since. Corinna still helps out with a slice of her paycheck, which is none too big. But me, man, I got horns, hoof, and tail. I eat babies for breakfast.

"Only lemme tell you something about Bruce. All the time he was so holy-holy, attending Mass every Sunday he was over on this side — but avoiding Communion, come to think of it — he didn't give a damn either. He just didn't have the nerve to make a clean break with those black crows, like me."

Kintyre, who had listened to many midnight hours of troubled young confidences, said quietly: "At the time he died, Bruce hadn't yet decided what he believed. He wouldn't hurt his parents for what might turn out to be a moment's intellectual whim."

"All right, all right. Only did you know he was shacking up?"

Kintyre raised his brows. "I'm surprised he told you. He introduced the girl around as his fiancée. In the apartment house he said she was his wife. He was more concerned about her reputation than she was."

"Come off it," snorted Guido. "Who did he fool?"

"Nnn ... nobody who met her, I suppose. He tried, but — "

"But this was the first woman he ever had, and it was such a big event he couldn't hide it. He was a lousy liar. Just for kicks, I badgered him till he broke down and admitted it to me."

"It was her idea," said Kintyre. "He wanted to marry her."

"Be this as it may," said Guido, "our little tin Jesus turns out to've been less than frank with everybody. So what else did he have cooking? Don't ask what I'm mixed up in. Look into his doings."

"I might," said Kintyre, "except that you have explained to me how poor a liar he was."

The girl came back with a pint of bourbon and a chit for Guido to sign. She leaned far over to set down a bottle of soda and two glasses of ice, so Kintyre could have a good look down her dress.

"Man," said Guido when she had oscillated off again, "Laura's got ants tonight. If you don't help yourself to that, I will."

"Why offer me the chance in the first place?" asked Kintyre. He ignored the proffered glass, sticking to his beer.

"I was going out on the town when I finished here. Know some places, they cost but they're worth it." Guido slugged his own glass full, added a dash of mix, and drank heartily. "They'll keep till tomorrow, though."

"I wonder where a chronically broke small-time entertainer gets money to splurge, all at once," said Kintyre.

Guido set his drink down again. Behind the loose, open blouse, his breast muscles grew taut.

"Never you mind," he said, in the bleakest voice Kintyre had yet heard him use. "Forget I mentioned it. Run along home and play with your books."

"As you wish. But when you're being officially grilled — and you will be, sonny — I wouldn't talk about Bruce in exactly the terms you used tonight. It sounds more and more as if you hated him."

Kintyre had no intention of leaving. Guido was disquietingly hard to understand. He might even, actually, be a party to the murder. Kintyre didn't want to believe that. He hoped all the tough and scornful words had been no more than a concealment, from Guido's own inward self, of bewildered pain. But he couldn't be sure.

He would have to learn more.

He sat back, easing his body, his mind, trying not to expect anything whatsoever. Then nothing could catch him off balance.

But the third party jarred him nonetheless.

A man came over toward the booth. He had evidently just made an inquiry of the waitress. He wore a good suit, painstakingly fashionable, and very tight black shoes. His face looked young.

Guido saw him coming and tightened fingers around his glass. A pulse in the singer's throat began to flutter.

"Get out," he said.

"What's wrong now?" Kintyre didn't move.

"Get out!" The eyes that turned to him were dark circles rimmed all around with white. The tones cracked across. "I'll see you later. There could be trouble if you stay. Blow!"

Kintyre made no doubt of it. Ordinarily he would have left, he was not one to search for a conflict. But he did not think any man could be worse to meet than the horror, and he could feel the horror still waiting to take him, as soon as he stopped having other matters to focus on.

He poured out the rest of his beer. Then the man was standing at the booth.

He was young indeed, Kintyre saw, perhaps so young he needed false identification to drink. His face was almost girlish, in a broad-nosed sleepy-eyed way, and very white. The rest of him was middling tall and well muscled; he moved with a sureness which told Kintyre he was quick on his feet.

"Uh," said Guido.

The young man jerked his head backward.

"He was just — just going," chattered Guido. "Right away."

"When I finish my beer, of course," said Kintyre mildly.

"Drink up," said the young man. He had no color in his voice. Its accent wasn't local, but Kintyre couldn't place the exact region. More or less Midwestern. Chicago?

It was a good excuse to get his back up. "I don't see where you have any authority in the matter," said Kintyre.

"Mother of God," whispered Guido frantically across the table. "Scram!"

The young man stood droop-lidded for a moment, considering. Then he said to Guido: "Okay. Another booth."

"Won't you join us here?" asked Kintyre. "You can say your say when I've gone."

The young man thought it over for a second or two. He shrugged faintly and sat down beside Kintyre, a couple of feet away. Shakily, Guido poured a drink into the unused glass of ice.

"Th-th-this is — Larkin," he said. "Terry Larkin. This is Professor Kintyre. He was a friend of my brother, is all."

"Are you from out of town, Mr. Larkin?" said Kintyre.

The young man took out a pack of cigarettes. It was the container for a standard brand, but the homemade cylinders inside were another matter. He lit one and sat back, unheeding of the whisky.

Kintyre would not have thought an ordinary drug addict anything to reckon with: the effects are too ruinous. But in spite of all the lurid stories, marijuana is a mild sort of dope, which leaves more control than alcohol and probably does less physiological damage than tobacco. If it came to trouble, Larkin was not going to be inconvenienced by a reefer or two.

"Friend of mine," said Guido. He was still tense, his smile a meaningless rictus. But a hope was becoming clear to see on him, that the episode would pass over quietly.

Kintyre did not mean for it to. There was more than coincidence here. If Larkin simply had private business to discuss, even illegal business, Guido would have had no reason to fear trouble. Larkin could merely wait until the professor took his bumbling presence home.

The trouble is, thought Kintyre, *I've been asking so many questions. I might irritate Happy here.*

Wherefore he dropped his bomb with some care: "Perhaps you can help me, Mr. Larkin. I suppose you know Guido's brother was murdered. Guido won't tell me where he was during that time, Saturday and Sunday, and I'm afraid he might get in trouble with the law."

Guido regarded Larkin like a beggar.

Larkin sat still. So still. It must have been half a minute before he moved. Then he looked through a woman's lashes at Kintyre and said:

"He was with me. We went out and picked daisies all weekend."

Kintyre smiled. "Well, if that's all — " His bomb had missed. He dropped another. "To avoid trouble, though, you'd better both go to the police with a statement."

"You're no cop," said Larkin.

"No. It was only a suggestion." Having bracketed the target, Kintyre dropped his third missile. "If they happen to ask me first what I know about it, I can refer them to you. Where are you staying?"

"*Gèsu Cristo,*" groaned Guido out of a lost childhood.

Larkin's face remained dead. But he laid down his cigarette and said slowly and clearly: "I told you to run along home. This time I mean it, daddy-o."

Kintyre bunched his muscles — only for an instant, then he remembered that he must be at ease, at ease.

"I'm beginning to wonder what you really were doing last weekend, Terry," he said.

There was hardly a visible movement. He heard the click, and the switchblade poised on the bench, aimed at his throat.

"End of the line," Larkin told him without rancor. "On your way. If you know what's good for you, you won't come back."

"Do you know," murmured Kintyre, "I think this really is a case for the police. Ever hear of citizen's arrest?"

Guido's wind rattled in his gullet.

Larkin's blade spurted upward. It was an expert, underhand sticking motion; Kintyre could have died with hardly a noise, in that booth designed not to be looked into from outside.

From the moment the steel emerged, he had realized he was going to get cut. That was half the technique of facing a knife. His last remark had been absolutely sincere: the law needed Larkin a prisoner, now. His left arm moved simultaneously with Larkin's right. The blade struck his forearm and furrowed keenly through the sleeve. It opened the skin beneath, but little more, for Kintyre was already lifting the arm, violently, as the follow-through slid Larkin's wrist across. He smacked the knife hand back against the booth wall.

His own right hand slipped under Larkin's knee. Then he half stood up; his left came down to assist; and he threw Larkin out of the booth.

He followed, out where there was room to deal properly with the boy. Larkin had hit a table (*Western movie style,* grinned part of Kintyre) and the whole business crashed and skated over the floor.

The bouncer ran ponderously to break up the fight. Kintyre had nothing against him, except that any delay would give Larkin too much time. He ran to meet the bouncer, therefore, stopped a fractional second before collision, and took the body's impact on his hip. It was elementary art from there on in. The bouncer bounced.

Larkin was back on his feet, spitting fury and blood. He'd lost his knife — should be easy to wrap up — *Hold it!*

The second switchblade gleamed among candles. Kintyre had almost impaled himself. He fell, in the judo manner, cushioned by an arm. Whetted metal buzzed where he had been. Rolling over on his back, Kintyre waited for Larkin to jump at him. Larkin was not that naïve. He picked a Chianti bottle off a table and threw it.

Kintyre saved his eyes with an arm hastily raised. The blow was numbing. He whipped to his feet again. The bartender circled on the fringes, gibbering and waving a bungstarter: the typical barroom fight is ridiculous, these two meant what they were doing. The bouncer dragged himself to his hands and knees.

"Call the police," snapped Kintyre. "And for God's sake, some of these tablecloths will start burning any minute!"

The customers were milling away. One of the fairies screamed; the butch stood on a chair and watched with dry avid eyes. Larkin backed off along the wall. Kintyre followed. Larkin wasn't foolish enough to rush; Kintyre would have to.

He waited till there was a small space clear of tables before him. Then he crouched low and ran in. His left arm was up, for a shield. He'd take that toadstabber in the biceps if he must.

Larkin, back against the bar, drew into himself. *Almost on one knee,* thought Kintyre as he plunged in, *like a Roman gladiator trying for the belly.* A tactical change was called for.

He shifted course and met the bar six feet from Larkin. His palms came down on it, he used his own speed to leap frogwise up to its surface, pivoting to face Larkin. He made one jump along the bar. His second was into the air. He landed with both feet on Larkin's back, before the other had more than half straightened.

Larkin went down, the knife flying from his hand. Kintyre fell off and went in a heap. This wasn't judo, it wasn't anything; Trig would laugh himself sick if he could watch. But —

Kintyre rolled back. Larkin was climbing unsteadily to his feet. Kintyre pulled him down and got a choking hold from behind. He lay on Larkin's back, his legs and sheer weight controlling the body, one arm around the throat, hands gripping wrists.

"Okay," he panted. "Squirm away. You'll just strangle yourself, you know."

Larkin hissed an obscenity. He was lighter, but Kintyre could feel a hard vitality in him. No matter, he was held now.

"Bartender," wheezed Kintyre. "Call the police — "

Something landed on his head.

It was like an explosion. For a moment he spiraled down toward night. He felt Larkin wriggle free, he groped mindlessly but his hands were empty and the world was blackness and great millstones.

Then he was aware once more. Guido crouched beside him, shaken and sobbing, and pawed at his bleeding scalp with a handkerchief. "Oh, God, Doc, I'm sorry, I'm sorry. Are you hurt?"

Kintyre looked around. "Where'd Junior go?" he croaked.

"Out the back door. Christ, Doc, I had to, you don't know what — Mary, Mother of God, forgive me, but — "

Kintyre stood up, leaning on Guido. A small riot was developing among the clientele and the help. He ignored it, brushing someone aside without even looking. The singer's stool lay at his feet. Guido must have clobbered him with that.

"Suppose you tell me why," he said.

"I — Get out. Get out before the cops come. I'll cover for you — tell them I don't know who you are, you were a stranger and — Get out!" Guido pushed at him, still weeping.

"I don't have anything to fear from them," said Kintyre. "It strikes me that maybe you do."

"Maybe," whispered Guido.

"Bruce died in a nasty way."

"This isn't — nothing to do with — I swear it, Doc, so help me God I do. Think I'd ever — It's something else, for Christ's sake!" Guido spoke in a slurred muted scream. "It's not only the cops I'm scared of, Doc, it's the others. They'd kill me!"

Kintyre studied him for a long second.

After all, he thought, this was Bruce's brother. And Corinna's.

"Okay," he said. "I promise you nothing. I, at least, will insist on knowing what this is all about. When I do, perhaps I'll decide the police ought to be told, and perhaps not. But for now, good night, Guido."

He turned to go out the rear exit. Faintly through the main door, he heard approaching sirens, but there was time enough to get into a back alley and thence to his car.

He realized, suddenly, with an unsurprised drowsy delight like the aftermath of love, that the horror had left him. When he continued his search for Larkin and for that more terrible thing which Larkin must represent, it would be from honor, because he was taking it on himself not to tell the police at once that there was a mansticker loose in their city. He would not be merely running from his private ghosts.

Tonight he would be able to sleep.

He paused at the door, looking back. "Good night, Guido," he repeated. "And thanks again for the song."

7

Two brawls in succession had not tired him; he got more exercise than that in an evening at the dojo. But the strain of the time before had had its effect. He woke with a fluttering gasp and saw dust motes dance in a yellow sunbeam. The clock said almost nine.

"Judas priest," he groaned. Suddenly it came to him that he had left Guido unguarded. So much for the amateur detective.

He sprang from bed and twirled the radio controls. Having found a newscast, he went into the bathroom and showered; Trig Yamamura had beaten that much Zen into his thick head. Through the water noise, he heard that more money was necessary so the nation's bought friends would stay bought; that the countries which had simply given their friendship were being imperialistic, i.e., hanging on to their overseas property, and therefore unworthy of help; that subversive elements in the bottle cap industry were to be investigated; and that Mother Bloor's Old Time Chicken Broth was made by a new scientific process which "sealed in" tiny drops of chicken goodness. Nothing was said about another murder.

Kintyre sighed and gave himself time to cook breakfast. If Guido hadn't been killed last night, he must be safely asleep at home by now. There were a few hours to spare.

He got into slacks and a gray sports shirt: he hated neckties and had no reason to wear one today. First, he decided, he must see Trig. After that he could wind up Bruce's University job. And, yes, he would take a closer look at the Book of Witches.

Yamamura's office was unimpressively above a drugstore in downtown Berkeley, a mile or so to walk. Kintyre found him polishing a Japanese sword. "Hi. Isn't this a nice one?" he boasted mildly. "I picked it up last week. It's only Tokugawa period, but get the heft, will you?"

Kintyre drew the blade. It came suddenly alive. He returned it with a faint sense of loss. "I could have used that chopper last night," he said.

"Yeh." Narrow black eyes drifted across him, the plaster high on his forehead and the outsize Band-Aid on his left forearm. "What happened, and is she going to prefer charges?"

"I suspect I met Bruce Lombardi's murderer," said Kintyre. "Or one of them."

Yamamura slid the sword carefully into its plain wooden scabbard. He took out his oldest briar and stuffed the bowl. Kintyre had finished his account by the time the pipe had a full head of steam up.

" — So I came on home."

Yamamura looked irritated. "It's your own stupid fault Larkin got away," he said. "Obviously you were holding your neck muscles tense. The stool wouldn't have hurt you to speak of if you weren't." He waggled his pipestem. "How often must I tell you, *relax*? Or don't you want to win your black belt?"

"Come off it," said Kintyre. "Look, what I'm afraid of is that Larkin, or someone associated with him, may decide Guido isn't safe to leave alive."

"All right. Let Guido ask the police for protection."

"He can't. I don't know why, but he doesn't dare. He'd rather take his chances with Larkin."

"I'd suggest that if he's that scared of the authorities, he deserves whatever he'll get."

"Don't be such a damned prig. Guido may be an accessory, of course, but I hate to think that. Why write him off before we're sure he wasn't just someone's dupe?"

"Mmmm. What has all this to do with me?"

"I want you to keep an eye on him."

"So? What's wrong with you doing this? Your vacation is coming up. I still have a living to make, and you can't pay me."

"I haven't the skill. And Guido and Larkin both know my face. Also, I do think I can be of some value on this side of the Bay."

"Huh! Sherlock Nero Poirot rides again."

"No. Think, Trig. The probability is that Bruce was killed by one or more professionals. But they didn't do it for fun. Somebody hired them, and that somebody is the real murderer. I've two reasons for wanting to meddle a little bit, rather than simply dumping what I know into the official lap. First, to spare Guido, at least till I'm sure if he's worth sparing or not. But second, this may not be entirely a police problem. They'll concentrate on the actual, physical killers, try to find one or two or three ants in the whole Bay Area antheap. They've no choice about that, it's their duty. Doubtless they'll put a man on the job of finding out who the killers' boss is. But the police don't know anyone concerned very intimately. The boss will have a certain amount of time to cover his tracks. Or to plan another murder.

"I knew Bruce well. I must have met all his friends, however casually. *I have met whoever had Bruce killed.* It may be sheer megalomania on my part, but I think there's a chance I could get an idea who it was."

Yamamura put his feet on the desk, leaned back, and stared out the window at the street. "Okay," he said at last. "On conditions."

"What?"

"I do have my family to keep. Not to mention my license. I'll undertake a week or so of Guido-guarding as an investment. Because if I could get a clue to the murderers, the boss or his torpedos, if I could give any substantial help to the police, the publicity would be good for my business. But to do anything useful along those lines, I'll have to leave Guido from time to time. I'll tail him when I think he may be in danger, yes, but when I think he's going to be safe for a few hours, I'll go check on something else."

"All right," said Kintyre. "In fact, excellent."

Yamamura looked at him through pipe smoke and said gravely: "If I find reasons why Guido should be arrested, I won't cover for him. I'll turn him in. Furthermore, I could make an error in judgment. I might leave Guido and come back to find Guido plus a knife. Now I sort of like you, Bob, don't ask me why. I'd hate to think you would hold either my informing or my mistake against me."

"Certainly not."

"Are you sure?"

"You know me, Trig."

Yamamura thought it over for a while. "Very well," he said. "Let's get the descriptions, addresses, and whatever else you know."

When they had finished, they were silent a few seconds.

"Oh, what did you find out about Owens?" asked Kintyre.

"Wife and two grown children in New York. Started as a business traveler, years ago; found that his hobby of writing paid more, and quit to write full time; captain's commission during the war, chairborne brigade in Washington —"

"If it takes a criminology degree to enter a bookstore, tell the clerk you're just looking, and read a dust jacket biography, then I'm in the wrong racket."

Yamamura settled himself more comfortably. "Owens has been hanging around Berkeley for several days without obvious motive," he said. "Addressed a writers' club Saturday night, but left early and was presumably on the town. They say at the hotel he slept late on Sunday, but no one remembers when he came in. Played some golf Sunday afternoon, dropped from sight again that night. Since then he's been simply — around. Bored, lonesome, but waiting for something or other."

"In short," said Kintyre, "it's possible he —"

"Did it personally? I don't know. Anything is possible, I guess. He may just have been out on the make, too. The chambermaid at his hotel tells me he's the pawing type. Of course, if the murder was done by proxy, these timetables don't mean anything anyway."

"Of course," said Kintyre.

8

Bruce had shared an office with four other assistants, but they were gone now. Bare of people, it had a hollow quality.

Kintyre went through the desk a final time. There was so little which was personally a man's. A few scrawls on the memo pad, a scratch sheet covered with intricate doodles, Margery's picture, some reference books, and a fat folder of notes relating to his research: no more. It could all be carried away in a single trip.

Kintyre attacked the remaining student papers. That was a mechanical task; few freshmen nowadays ever showed much originality, except in their spelling. Most of his brain idled. It occurred to him that one common element bound together everyone who seemed to figure in this affair. The Italian nation and culture.

Angelo, Maria, Guido Lombardi: All born in Genoa.

Bruce Lombardi: Born over here, but oriented toward the old country, writing his master's thesis as a critical exegesis of a medieval Italian manuscript, corresponding with an uncle in the Italian secret service.

Corinna Lombardi: Well, Bruce's sister; spoke the language too.

Margery Towne: Bruce's girl. Admittedly a weak connection.

Himself, Robert Kintyre: Postgraduate studies of the Renaissance, on a fellowship which kept him in Italy from 1949 to 1951; took his Ph.D. at Cal with a study of those lesser known sociological writings before Machiavelli which had influenced the Florentine realist; returned overseas for a year ending last summer, on another grant to continue his researches; now teaching and working on a book which only specialists would ever read.

Jabez Owens: Visited Europe, including Italy, many times. Claimed, as a semiamateur scholar, to have unearthed some lurid Borgia correspondence, which he had turned to his own profit.

Gerald Clayton: Officer in the Army Quartermaster Corps in Italy, during the latter part of the war. Returned there immediately after his discharge, came back in a couple of years with the American franchise for a new line of Italian motor scooters. Since then he spent half his time abroad, pumping a steadily larger flow of European goods into the United States market, everything from automobiles to perfumes. Also interested in manuscripts. Had several tracked down for him by Italian scholars, bought them, sent them home. He obtained the Book of Witches in Sicily, and carried it along when business took him to San Francisco last fall. Found Kintyre was the man to see, looked him up, asked him to examine the volume for whatever value it had. Kintyre had turned the project over to Bruce; it would make a good M.A. thesis. Clayton had pungled up a couple of thousand dollars as a research grant: a graceful way of making it financially possible for Bruce to give some time to the task. Since then Clayton had frequently seen both Bruce and Kintyre, and shown a real if not very deep interest in the boy's progress.

Gene Michaelis: Served his Navy hitch in the Mediterranean theater. Yes, Bruce had mentioned that. What might have happened during Gene's Italian shore leaves was an intriguing question.

Peter Michaelis: Gene's father, as embittered as he toward the Lombardi tribe.

Terry Larkin: No connection demonstrated, but it was quite possible in this land of many races.

"Holy Hieronymus," muttered Kintyre, "next thing I'll be looking for a Black Hand."

But melodramatic and implausible facts were still stubbornly facts.

He completed his task about noon, turned in the papers and reports, and got the Book of Witches from the department safe. He wanted a better acquaintance with this thing.

Bruce's office was too empty. He took the manuscript and the folder of notes to his own room. It was just as bare and quiet between these walls, but more familiar. He could look out the window to lawns and blowing trees and sunlight spilling over them — without thinking that Bruce lay frozen under a sheet.

He put the book on his desk with care. It was almost six hundred years old.

The phone rang. He jerked in surprise, swore at himself, and picked it up. "Hello?"

"Kintyre? Jabez Owens."

"Oh. What is it?"

"I called your home and you weren't in, so I tried — How are you?"

"I'll live. What's the occasion?"

"I wondered — I'd like to talk to you. Would you care to have lunch with me?"

"No, thanks." Kintyre had better plans than to watch Owens perform. "I'm busy."

"Are you sure?" The voice was worried.

"Quite. I'll be here for some hours. I'll just duck out for a sandwich." Maliciously: "I've some work to do on Bruce's project. Afterward — "

What? Well, he hadn't called Margery today. He supposed, with a faintly suffocated feeling, that he ought to see her. "I have an engagement," he finished.

"Oh." Hesitantly: "Do you think I could drop up to your office, then? It really is urgent, and it may be to your own advantage."

"Sure," said Kintyre, remembering his wish to play sleuth. "Walk into my parlor." He gave Owens the room number and hung up. Then he returned to the Book of Witches.

It was a thick palimpsest, a little over quarto size. The binding, age-eaten leather with rusted iron straps, was perhaps a century newer than the volume itself. He opened it, heavy in his hands, and looked at the title page. *Liber Veneficarum* —

Book of Witches, Their Works and Days, Compiled from Records and the Accounts of Trustworthy Men, Done at the Sicilian Abbey of St. John the Divine at the Command of the Abbot Rogero, for the Attention and Use of the Authorities of Our Holy Mother Church.

When Clayton first brought it around, Kintyre had only skimmed through the black uncials in a hasty fashion. He knew there had been considerable Satanism in the Middle Ages, partly pagan survivals and partly social protest, but that had not seemed to be in his immediate line. A man has only time to learn a few things before the darkness takes him back.

Now he opened Bruce's folder and began to read the notes. Some were typewritten, some still in pothooks harder to decipher than the fourteenth century Low Latin. But they were in order, and their own references were clearly shown. Bruce had been a good, careful scholar.

Well — Kintyre turned to the first page. It was very plain work, unilluminated. The opening sentences described the purpose: to set forth exactly what the witchcraft movement was, how widespread and how dangerous to the Faith and the state. Sources were given, with some commentary on their trustworthiness. The Middle Ages did not lack critical sense. The monk wrote soberly of witchcraft as a set of real activities in the real world; he wasted very little time on the demons presumed to be the object of worship.

Kintyre struggled with his memory, brought back an approximate recollection of a later passage, and hunted for it again. Yes, here, near the middle: an account of a thirteenth century witch hunt in northern Italy, a follow-up to the Albigensian Crusade. The author said that since then there had been no covens worth mentioning north of Abruzzi, and cited proof — statements by Church and secular investigators, a couple of confessions extracted by torture.

Bruce's notes at this point gave confirming cross references. A penciled afterthought occurred: "If there were no organized Satanists in the Romagna in 1398, it hardly seems reasonable that Cesare Borgia could have joined them a century later!" Evidence was marshaled to show there had been no revival in the meantime. Rather, the cults had been on the wane throughout the fifteenth century, as prosperity and enlightenment spread.

Well, thought Kintyre, *that does pretty well sink Owens' boat.*

Something caught his eye. He leaned over the sheet. A fifteenth century "discourse," an official report, in the state archives of Milan was quoted to support the claim that there was no contemporary local Black Mass. In the margin was scribbled "L.L."

Private abbreviations could be weird and wonderful, but Kintyre found himself obscurely irritated. So much was unknown about Bruce's final destiny, even an initial might tell something.

He found the letters several times more in the next hour, as he worked his way through the volume and the notes. They seemed to mark findings which could only be made in Italy: by going out and looking at a site, or by reading in ancient libraries.

The telephone interrupted him again. He glanced at his watch. Two o'clock already! He grew aware that he was hungry.

"Hello. Robert Kintyre speaking."

The voice in his ear was low. It stumbled the barest bit. "Professor Kintyre. This is Corinna Lombardi."

"Oh." He sat gaping into the mouthpiece like a schoolboy, feeling his heartbeat pick up. "Oh, yes," he said stupidly.

"I wanted to apologize to you."

"Hm?" With an effort, he pulled himself toward sense. "What the dev — What in the world is there to apologize for?"

"Last night. I was horrible."

Habit took over, the smoothness of having known many women; but his tone was burred. "Oh, now, please don't be silly. If you won't mind my saying so at a time like this, I thought you were quite extraordinarily pleasant to meet."

Did he catch the unsubstantial wisp of a chuckle? "Thank you. You're very kind. But I did pull a regular Lady Macbeth. It was nerves. I was tired and miserable. I hope you'll believe how sorry I've been all day. I've spent the past half hour at the phone, trying to track you down."

"If I'd known that, I'd have laid a paper trail — Blast!" Kintyre checked himself. "Now it's my turn to ask your pardon. I wasn't thinking."

"It's all right," she said gently.

"No, but — "

"Really it is. Now that the requiem Mass has been held, the solemn one Mother wanted — it was almost like a real funeral. Everything looks different now."

"Yes, I saw the announcement. I couldn't come, I had to finish his work."

"I could envy you that," she said. Then, with a lifting in her tone: "I came back and slept. I woke up only an hour ago. It's like a curtain falling. Bruce is dead, and that will always hurt, but we can go on now with our own lives."

He hovered on the edge of decision, wondering what to do, afraid of the ghoul she might think him. A line from *The Prince* came: "*... it is better to be impetuous than cautious, for fortune is a woman* — " All right, he told himself.

"There's one thing, Miss Lombardi."

"Yes?" She waited patiently for him to sort out his words.

"I haven't forgotten what you did say last night. I went ahead and looked into it, your ideas, I mean."

"Oh?" A noncommittal noise, not openly skeptical.

"I can tell you something you may feel better for."

"What?" Caution, now, not of him but of the thing he might say.

"The phone is hardly suitable. Could we get together in person?"

"Well — " It stretched into seconds, which he found unnaturally long. Then, clearly, almost gaily: "Of course. Whenever you like."

"This evening? You're at your parents' home still, aren't you?"

"I'm going back to my own place today. But this evening will be fine."

He said with careful dryness: "Bearing in mind that I am a somewhat respectable assistant professor of history and more than a decade your senior, may I suggest dinner?"

She did actually chuckle that time. "Thank you, you may. No references needed; Bruce told me enough about you. And it's a good deal better than sitting alone brooding, isn't it?"

He had gotten the address and a six-thirty date before he wholly realized what was going on. When the phone was back in its cradle, he sat for some indefinite time. *Oh, no!* he thought at last. *Impossible. I'm too old to be romantic and too young to be tired.*

He decided to eat before going back to the manuscript.

While he went out for a sandwich and milkshake, while he walked back again, he twisted his attention to the problem of the book. It could have wrought a man's death, or it could only be a stack of inked parchment. Most likely the latter; but then who or what was L. L.?

The building was gloomy when he re-entered it from sunlight. Even his office seemed dark. It took his eyes a few seconds to register the fact that the book was gone.

9

Kintyre stood for a little while more, scarcely thinking.

Then, during an instant, he had a vision of tiny black devils fluttering through the half-open window, lifting the volume and squeaking their way out on quick charred wings. But no, no, this was the twentieth century. We are rational, we don't believe in witchcraft, we are scientific and believe in vitamin pills, Teamwork, and the inalienable right of every language to have a country of its own. Also, the phase of the moon was wrong, and — and —

His mind steadied. He whirled about the desk, to see if the book had somehow slid off. No. He snatched up the phone and called the main office. Had anyone come into his room in the past twenty minutes? We don't know, Dr. Kintyre. No, we did not pick up your book. No, we didn't see anyone.

He put back the instrument and tried to start his thoughts. It was curiously hard. He tended to repeat himself. Someone must have come in. Yes, someone must have come in. It would be easy to do, unobserved. Someone must have come in and taken the book.

What the hell had Margery's apartment been burgled for?

That snapped him back to wakefulness. If, as Clayton had suggested yesterday, the burglar was after this volume and hadn't found it, the University was the next logical place to try.

Owens! I told him I'd go out to eat. He could have watched the entrance.

But where was he now? — Wait. Close your eyes, let the mind float free, don't strain too hard — memory bobbed to the surface. Owens had mentioned taking a room in the Bishop, a hotel conveniently near campus.

Kintyre forced himself into steadiness. If Owens had copped the book, Owens would want to get rid of it. Permanently. But leather and parchment don't burn easily. Dumping it meant too much chance of its being noticed and recovered. Owens would take it to Los Angeles with him, to destroy at leisure.

He was probably packing at this moment.

Kintyre tucked Bruce's notes into a drawer which he locked: not that they had any value without the physical evidence of the book. He went down the hall fast, a pace he kept up on the outside. His brain querned until he brought it under control. Damn it, Trig was right, there was no reason on God's earth ever to tense any muscle not actually working; and the same held true for the mind. An emotional stew would grind him down and get him to the Bishop no sooner.

It was a hard discipline, though. Kintyre had no urge to embrace Zen Buddhism, or any other faith for that matter; but he would have given much to possess the self-mastery it taught.

He entered the modest red-brick building a few blocks from Sather Gate and asked for Mr. Owens. The clerk checked the key rack and said: "Oh, yes, he came in a few minutes ago."

"I'll go on up, I'm expected," said Kintyre. It was probably not a lie.

When he knocked on the writer's door, he heard himself invited in. Owens had one suitcase open on the bed and was folding a coat into it. Another stood strapped on the floor.

He looked up (was his color a shade more rubicund?) and said, "Hullo, there. I'm glad you came by. I'm leaving tonight."

The voice was level. Perhaps too level. Kintyre closed the door and said: "I thought you were going to come and see me in my office."

"Well, I was," said Owens. "I wanted to get my packing out of the way first." He felt in the suitcase and brought out a pocket flask. "Care for a drop?"

"No," said Kintyre.

He leaned in the doorway, watching. But he saw only that Owens stood neatly attired, calm of face, steady of hands, putting up a linen suit.

"What brings you here?" asked the writer.

Kintyre countered: "Isn't this a rather sudden decision to leave?"

"Mm, yes. I made the reservation just a few minutes ago. But I haven't much reason to stay here any longer, have I?"

"The Lombardi murder."

Owens shook his head. "Poor chap. But what can I do about it? I assure you, the police didn't ask me to stay in town."

He gave Kintyre a straight look, smiled, and went on: "Why don't you sit down and talk to me, though? I'm more or less stuck till Clayton arrives. He said he'd meet me here."

"Clayton? Why — " Kintyre moved slowly forward, to the armchair Owens waved at. He continued talking, inanely. "I thought Clayton was in the City. He told me yesterday when we had lunch, he told me he'd be going right over there and didn't expect to come back to this side in the near future."

"Oh? I called him at the Fairhill, just before you got here. He was right in his suite."

Kintyre sat down. "What did you want him for?"

"To make him an offer for the Book of Witches."

"What!"

"Take it easy," advised Owens. "You don't own the thing."

The effort not to pounce left Kintyre rigid. He managed finally to say: "I suppose that was what you wanted to see me about, to offer me the same bribe Bruce wouldn't take."

"I see you've gotten a somewhat biased version." Owens' reply had the blandness of conscious mastery. "Yes, it was to be a similar offer. Not that I don't stand behind my contentions in the Borgia matter, but you people in this academic cloudland don't realize that the rest of us have a living to make. I have no time at present to dig into minutiae, and anyhow there are more important things in life. What I asked Lombardi was that he postpone the argument. Not perjure his precious self, only wait a while. There were enough other things to be written about, anent that book. He didn't have to raise the Borgia issue at all. Maybe in five or ten years — "

"Since you brought up the Borgia issue, as you call it, in the first place," said Kintyre harshly, "we in cloudland have no choice. If there's a notorious error afoot, we've got to correct it. What the hell do you think we get paid for?"

"Publicity," said Owens. "Ornament. A ritual bow in the direction of yesterday." He took forth a silver case, opened it, fetched out a long cigarette and tapped it on his thumbnail.

"You claim to be a realist," he said. "Then why don't you admit the facts? This business of scholarship, verification, the painful asymptotic approach to truth — it's dead. It went out with the society of aristocrats. This is a proletarian age." He lit the cigarette. His trained lecture-circuit voice rolled out, urbane, whimsical, with a bare touch of sadness. "He who dances must pay the piper, but he who pays the piper may call the tune. Since the bills today are all being footed by slobs, what do you expect but the onward march of slobbery? One day you'll be fired in the name of government economy. I'll hang on a little longer, because I gauge the current level of oafishness and make each succeeding book conform; but sooner or later it will be too much trouble for the public even to read my swill. Then I'll settle down to live on my investments, and perhaps I can even go back to a little honest scholarship. But not now. First I must survive."

Kintyre said slowly, caught up in spite of himself: "Granted, this is the century of the common mind. But what makes you think it will last, even long enough for you to collect on those investments? This is also the so-called atomic age."

Owens lifted his shoulders and let them fall again, gracefully. "How do I know I won't be hit by a car tomorrow? One estimates the situation and acts on probabilities."

Kintyre leaned forward. "The probabilities are all for the worst," he said. "Anyone who claims a roomful of people, all with grenades and all hating each other, will keep on acting rationally forever, is whistling past the graveyard of a dozen earlier civilizations. But I do believe scholarship — rigorous thinking — will be a survival factor. And afterward it will be one of the things which will make cultural rebuilding worth while. So I won't quit trying. It isn't for nothing."

He stood up, not as tall as Owens, but broader and smoothly moving. "Let me therefore have that manuscript back," he finished.

His enemy kept a half smile; but as he neared, Kintyre saw how cheeks and forehead began to glisten. The pupils that stared at him widened until they were two wells of dark.

"What are you talking about?" said Owens shrilly.

"You know bloody damn well what I mean. You took the Book of Witches. Give it back and we'll say no more. Otherwise — "

Kintyre was almost upon the writer. Owens backed away, holding up his cigarette like a futile sword. "Look here," he protested. "Look here, now."

There came a rap on the door. Owens went limp with relief. "Come in!" he yelled.

Kintyre realized bitterly how he had been snared. Owens had thrown out words which he knew the other must stop to answer. It had gained him a few seconds that might well make his victory; Kintyre took him for a physical coward who would not have stood up long even to verbal browbeating.

Or did I actually intend to wring it from him with my hands? The thought was so shocking that Kintyre stepped back.

Gerald Clayton entered, massive in gray, his narrow face wearing only a routine smile. It became more nearly genuine when he saw Kintyre. "Why, hello, there," he said. "What's going on?"

Owens threw his opponent a look. *If you don't say anything about this, I won't.* Kintyre held himself expressionless, waiting.

"Sit down, Mr. Clayton, do sit down." Owens gestured him to a chair. "I appreciate your coming. I know your time is valuable."

The importer seated himself and took out a cigar. Owens hovered around with his pocket flask; the drink was declined. Kintyre leaned against the wall, arms folded, and strove for calm.

"I wasn't very busy," said Clayton. "Glad of a chance to get away, in fact." He nodded at Kintyre and explained: "Something came up which forces me to stay in Berkeley at least till tomorrow. But it involves mostly waiting till I can see the person in question. So what did you want, Jabez?"

Owens shot another glance at Kintyre, gathered himself, and said: "I wondered if you'd be interested in selling the *Liber Veneficarum?*"

Clayton's mouth bent upward, creasing his lean cheeks. "Whatever for?" he asked, almost merrily. "I'm a collector."

"Well." Owens sat down on the bed, more at ease now. "You're aware of my argument with Bruce Lombardi. I admit it's possible I was cheated on those letters — " *or commissioned the forgeries yourself,* reflected Kintyre — "and if not, at least the case against me deserves careful refutation. So I would like to have the manuscript, to study at my own leisure."

"And never get around to publishing your findings?" asked Clayton. But he said it in a twitting, inoffensive tone.

"It might take me a few years," said Owens doggedly. "I've other work to do. However, I'm prepared to make a fair offer for the book. Or, if you don't want to sell, I would like to borrow it for a year or two, under suitable guarantees against loss."

Clayton rubbed his chin. "Seems to me that Bob has some rights in this matter," he declared.

Kintyre stepped a pace forward. His voice snapped out: "The reason I came here is that the manuscript was stolen from me."

"What?" Clayton shouted it, half rose, sat down again and puffed hard at his cigar. "What happened?" he said roughly.

Kintyre related the morning. "It fits pretty well," he concluded. "First he plans an attempt to bribe me, as he tried to bribe Bruce. Did you know he offered Bruce five thousand dollars to withhold his findings? I mention on the phone I'll be going out to lunch. Since he doesn't really expect I'll bribe either, Owens hangs around. When he sees me leave, he ducks up into my office. If the book isn't there, he can always try the original scheme. But it's right on my desk, and I apologize for my own carelessness. Owens takes it back here. Then, to cover himself, he phones you with this offer to buy — as if he didn't know it was gone!"

Kintyre finished in a growl: "That suitcase on the floor, already packed, would hold a quarto volume very easily."

Clayton remained impassive.

The writer said with strained calm: "I ask you to witness this, sir. I'm thinking of a suit for slander."

"That book is worth enough to make it theft grand larceny," said Clayton.

"And what alibi does the good Professor Kintyre have?" flung Owens.

"Who but you has a motive for the book to disappear?" said Kintyre. "By God — "

Owens got off the bed and retreated again. Kintyre strode up to him and laid a hand about his wrist. He did not squeeze unduly hard, but Owens opened his mouth to scream, face going paper colored. Kintyre dropped the wrist as if it had turned incandescent. The reaction was unnatural enough, to his mind, to jar him physically.

"That'll do!" rumbled Clayton. He stood up. His grizzled ruddy hair made Kintyre think of a lion's mane, a fighting cock's comb; this man had slugged his own way up from nothingness.

"That'll do," he repeated. "If we can't settle it between ourselves like gentlemen, we'd better call the police."

Owens fumbled his way to the pocket flask, raised it and gulped. A little blood returned to his skin. "I thought you were going to hit me," he said in a tiny voice. "I never could — "

"Owens," said Clayton, "did you steal the book?" His tone fell like iron.

"No." The writer put his flask down on the bureau. He remained standing above it, leaning on his hands, looking back over a hunched shoulder. "No, of course not."

"Mind if we look around to make sure?"

"I don't wish my baggage opened," said Owens. "You haven't the right."

Kintyre, with a measure of control restored to him, said: "We could prefer charges and have the police look."

"Go ahead," said Owens more firmly. "I'll sue you for every nickel you've got. I'd enjoy that."

"I don't like trouble," said Clayton. "If you have the book, return it. We'll say you — borrowed it — nobody else ever has to hear a word."

Owens whirled around. "That's a reflection on my integrity!" he shouted.

"If you really are innocent," said Clayton in a patient way, "I should think you'd want your integrity confirmed."

Owens studied them for a moment.

"All right," he said. "I don't blame you, Mr. Clayton. Your reaction is very understandable. But this character — Mr. Clayton, in case I decide to sue him, and I probably will, remember exactly what happened today. Now go ahead and search."

The importer squatted by the suitcase. It didn't take him long to go through the neatly packed clothing. There was no book.

10

"Somewhere else," mumbled Kintyre. "Under the bed."

"Stand aside," said Clayton.

He went to work, peering, poking, moving about the room and its bath like a professional. He found places to check which Kintyre would not have thought of in a week's hunt; and yet the broad ropy-veined hands, which had once wielded a shovel, made little disarrangement.

Owens sat down, poured himself another drink, and sipped as if it were victory he tasted. Kintyre stood by the window sill, wrestling himself toward calm. He had not yet fully achieved it when Clayton said: "Not in here."

"Well," murmured Owens.

Clayton puffed blue smoke, sat down on the bed, and gave them both a quizzical glance. "I suppose an apology is in order," he said.

Owens waved his cigarette. "Look," he replied, giving it the complete treatment, "I've cooled off a bit myself. I can see how you were overwrought, Professor, from the death of your friend — and, to be sure, the loss of a valuable relic entrusted to you." Kintyre held his mouth stiff. "If you'll take this as a lesson, I for my part am willing to forget it."

"You might thank the man, Bob," added Clayton lightly.

Kintyre grunted. What could you say?

"It's worth while reviewing the facts, though," went on Clayton. "Maybe between us we can figure who did swipe it."

"No students around," said Owens.

"True. But anybody could have lounged outside till Bob left and then walked up into his office, without much risk of being seen. Right?"

Kintyre nodded. His neck ached with tension.

"Okay." Clayton blew a smoke ring. "I guess we can rule out an ordinary thief. He wouldn't pick a college building. How about other people with offices there?"

Kintyre stirred. "Now, wait," he began.

Clayton waved him back. "Take it easy, Bob. Just for the record, is anybody but you working in that place between sessions?"

"Well, some," he forced himself to say. "It's a sizable department. And then the clerical staff, and janitors. But for God's sake!"

"Their own office doors wouldn't be locked, though?"

"Hm? No, I suppose not. At least, a number wouldn't be. Even if they weren't in today, there'd be nothing to steal."

"Except manuscripts." Owens had been seated, listening with a tolerant smile. Now he said in a cool voice, "Not to follow the recent bad example of accusations, but what *is* your alibi, Kintyre?"

"No motive!"

"Oh? I daresay there are other wealthy collectors besides Mr. Clayton. With your contacts, you could have learned who they are. Mind you, I don't charge you with anything, but — "

"Cut it out," interrupted Clayton. It was so cold a phrase that they both turned startled faces to him.

He got up. "This farce has gone on long enough," he said. "Jabez, give me my book."

"What?" Owens leaned away. Clayton walked toward him. Owens lifted a fending arm.

"I don't feel like hunting through a lot of rooms for it," said Clayton. "Which did you leave it in?"

"But — but — but — "

"Do I have to spell it out? It's plain to see, either you or Bob took the thing. Who the hell else is there? I credit Bob with brains enough to steal it more neatly. Like setting an 'accidental' fire he could tell me burned it. You had to work fast, though. Play by ear. You grabbed it exactly as Bob thought. Only you realized he'd come back in a few minutes and go howling on your trail. What better way to throw him off it than to let him make a fool of himself before me — me, the owner, who's really got a right to blow his stack?"

Clayton stood over Owens with the big fists on his hips, beating him about the head with words. "You left it in one of those empty offices, or maybe in the can. They won't lock the main entrance till five o'clock or so, I guess. You could have picked the thing up again at your convenience, when Bob had gone off with his tail between his legs. It was fun while it lasted, Jabez, but now suppose you tell me where that book is."

"I didn't!" screamed Owens.

"I don't want to press charges," said Clayton. "Tell me, and we'll call it quits. Otherwise we can all wait right here for the police."

Owens began to shake. Kintyre looked away, feeling a little sick himself. "All right," said Clayton and picked up the phone.

"No," whimpered Owens. "Don't."

"Well?" Clayton paused, one finger in a dial hole.

Owens got out a room number. "Under the desk," he added, and lowered his face into his hands.

"Can we check that from here?" asked Clayton.

Kintyre nodded, took the phone and called the department. He asked one of the girls to look, feeding her a story about having lent the volume out. Then he held the line and waited.

"Well," said Clayton. He drew on his cigar, relaxed visibly, and laughed. "Maybe I ought to set up as a private eye. Know any hard-boiled blondes?"

"Nice work," said Kintyre inadequately. "Good Lord, if that book really had been lost!"

"It wouldn't have been your fault," said Clayton. "Forget it."

Kintyre looked down at a shuddering back. "It seems to be my turn now, Owens," he said. "No hard feelings. *Va' tu con Dio.*"

"No," said Clayton. "I'm afraid not."

Kintyre stared up again, into the narrow face and the deeply ridged eyes. "I thought," he said, "I thought you wouldn't — "

"Prefer charges? Not about a lousy manuscript. My time's worth too much. But Bruce Lombardi was murdered, remember?"

Owens lifted a seared countenance and gasped: "No, you can spare me that much, can't you?"

"I hope so," said Clayton impersonally. "But the fact remains, Bruce was a threat to a fat piece of Hollywood cash."

"He was going to expose the Borgia fraud publicly, as well as in specialized journals," said Kintyre, not wanting to.

"That made it even more urgent," said Clayton. "If Bruce should die and the book disappear, I don't know who'd stand to benefit more than you."

Owens emitted a little moaning noise and shriveled back into the mask of his hands. "You see?" said Clayton.

"Wait," protested Kintyre. "I can't really believe he — "

"I'm open to proof," said Clayton.

Kintyre fell silent.

After a while the girl's voice said in the phone: "I found it, Dr. Kintyre. Right where you told me."

"Thanks a lot," he answered automatically. "Would you put it in the safe?" He nodded and hung up.

"Good," said Clayton. He spoke slowly and carefully to Owens' bent head: "We'll leave now. You stay around Berkeley for a while. I'm going to have to call your motive to the attention of the police, so if you left there'd probably be a warrant for you by tonight. But I won't say anything about your peccadillo this afternoon. And if you're innocent, I recommend that you start scrounging around for witnesses to where you were all weekend."

"Whoof!" said Kintyre when he was in the lobby. "I wouldn't like to go through that again."

"Nor I," said Clayton. "Let's have something wet."

They went into the coffee shop and ordered. Kintyre said: "Owens didn't do the murder. I doubt if he's capable of killing his own flies."

"Himself," said Clayton shortly. "He could have hired a torpedo. He's got money enough. Not that killers come fabulously expensive."

Almost, Kintyre told him of last night. He stopped with the words at his teeth. After this hour's performance, it seemed too probable that Clayton would insist on telling the San Francisco authorities about Larkin, on the instant, and the consequences to Guido (and thereby to Guido's parents and Corinna) go hang.

As far as that goes, I suppose I've made myself an accessory after the fact or something.

They remained in a companionable silence until the coffee had arrived. It was refreshing to know an unfrantic businessman; but then, Clayton had acquired a lot of European traits.

The importer asked suddenly: "Have you seen Miss Towne?"

"Not today," said Kintyre, surprised.

"Were you planning to?"

"Why — yes. I thought I'd drop around this afternoon. She told me she didn't feel up to working for the rest of this week."

"It might be better if she did," said Clayton. "She'll sit at home and grieve, or go out and laugh more than she means. Drinking too much in either case."

"You seem to know her pretty well," said Kintyre. He felt a bit annoyed, he didn't know why.

"I met her a few times is all. But she's pretty transparent, under all that careful sophistication, isn't she?" Clayton stirred his coffee, focusing on the spoon as if it were some precision instrument. "A good kid."

"She's all right," said Kintyre.

"I suppose you feel an obligation toward her?"

Kintyre bridled. "I didn't mean to keyhole," said Clayton hurriedly. "I just couldn't help wondering what'll become of her. Somebody has to help her over the hump. She'll never make it alone."

Against his own principles of respect for privacy, Kintyre found himself speculating. Where had Clayton picked up such intuitions? His first wife, whom he had loved, seemed by his few chance remarks and his *Who's Who* biography to have been the conventional helpmeet of a conventional young man in the thirties: grocery clerk, salesman, pitchforked down by the Depression, up again via WPA to construction foreman to warehouse foreman to minor executive. Finally she got tuberculosis, with complications, and took a couple of years to die. The medical bills ruined him; he parked the three children with relatives for years. Afterward, on the way up once more in the defense boom and the early war boom, he married the boss's daughter. He got to be general superintendent of an aircraft plant before he learned what a bitch she was. The divorce cost him that job and his savings. He applied for an Army commission and got one in 1943.

Kintyre knew little else; his information was only the gossip one is bound to encounter. Clayton had been a fairly large figure in Italy when Kintyre went over for the second time.

"Eh?" he said, pulled back to awareness.

"I asked if you wanted to take her out tonight," repeated Clayton.

"Uh — "

"Somebody ought to." As if he had heard Kintyre's thoughts, Clayton said with an enormous gentleness: "She reminds me a lot of my daughter."

Clayton had never had any great chance to be a father, reflected Kintyre. After the war, his kids ended up in exclusive boarding schools while Dad was overseas reaping the money to keep them there. Now they were grown. The girl had been graduated last year and was still making her Grand Tour. Clayton sometimes bragged about her, in clumsy generalities: he scarcely knew her as a person. The second son was also worth a cautious boast or two, apparently a solid-citizen type, an engineer; he and his father doubtless exchanged very dutiful letters. The older boy, you didn't hear much about. You got an impression of a sinecure in the firm's New York office and divorce number three currently going through the mill.

Kintyre wondered, suddenly, if he had ever known anyone more alone than Clayton.

It came to him that an answer was expected. "No," he said, "I have another engagement this evening."

"Not one you could break? She does need help."

"So does Miss Lombardi. Bruce's sister. I have some news for her that could make a big difference."

Clayton paused a moment. Then he grinned. "Well, in that case," he said, "d'you mind if I squire Miss Towne?"

Kintyre looked up, startled. He had been slipping into a mood of utter oleaginous sentimentalism. Pity Clayton? The hell! You wouldn't think the man was past forty. He sat there with more life in his eyes than two buccaneer captains.

"Good heavens, no," exclaimed Kintyre. "Why ever should I?"

Margery could do a lot worse, he thought. He knew his eagerness was chiefly to get rid of whatever responsibility he bore for her. Nevertheless — *A lot worse!*

It was after four when Kintyre entered Margery's apartment. She had neglected its housekeeping, and the air was acrid with smoke.

Slacks and sweater emphasized her figure. He had almost forgotten how good it was. When she sprang from the couch and into his arms he found himself kissing her without really having intended to.

"Oh, God, Bob," she whispered. "You came. Hold me close, kiss me again, I need it."

Her nails dug into his flesh, painfully, and her lips were tense against his. And yet it was but little a sexual passion, he realized; she was altogether forlorn.

"Rough?" he asked. He freed one arm and rumpled the short coppery hair.

"Reporters," she said. "Waiting at the door when I came home today. Like flies around a corpse."

The phone rang. She left it alone; the bell had been turned down. "Most likely someone else panting to pry," she said.

"How — oh, yes," said Kintyre. "The burglary would put them on to it. Or just asking around. You didn't really think your connection with Bruce would escape discovery forever?"

"It'll be smeared over every newsstand in the area. Big black mouth-licking headlines." She raised reddened eyes. "I was at the service this morning. It was all so calm and — I don't know — so right. Even for him." She pulled herself away, picked up a handkerchief and blew her nose. "Excuse me. I can't help it. That was the only sane part of the day. His parents were there, of course, that decent old couple. I didn't have the nerve to talk to them. And now they'll see! They'll know that every moron in town knows their son they were so proud of was, was, with me!"

She fell into a chair, coughing. The phone stopped its petulance.

Kintyre said: "After all, pony, it's no crime in this state. Nor is it a very black sin in the Church. I wouldn't be at all surprised if the Lombardis got in touch with you in the friendliest way. If you loved Bruce too — "

"Did I?" She didn't look at him. "I liked him, yes, but love? Not in the usual sense of the word."

"Which is a pretty neurotic sense anyway, if you're past adolescence," said Kintyre in his driest voice.

She had regained her balance. She reached for a compact and began repairing her makeup. "Bob," she said, "for an intelligent man you can make some of the stupidest remarks on record."

Kintyre smiled. "At least I riled you out of a tailspin." He wandered across the room to the coffee table. An empty cup and an ashtray overflowing with lipsticked butts rested by the long cardboard boxes where Bruce had kept his letters. They were open, and one of the sheets lay out.

Margery came over and took his arm. "I was going through it," she said, suddenly anxious for the everyday. "Mostly it was business correspondence, official papers, that sort of thing. But there's one file in Italian. Maybe you can tell me what it means." The phone buzzed. "Shut up, God damn it!"

Kintyre sat down, taking out a cigarette for himself. He did not quite like reading a dead man's mail. But doubtless it had to be done. "I'll make some more coffee," said Margery. She went out to the kitchen; his eyes shifted in her direction and he felt the animal pleasure of watching her walk. It was possible — once more, after a decent interval?

Then he realized that the lilt within him was because he would be seeing Corinna.

He bent his attention to the file. Sloppy in many other respects, Bruce had been meticulous here. If it was likely to have any future value at all, he typed his own letter, making a carbon for himself, and kept the reply, folded. The section indexed *Luigi Lombardi* held at least a year's worth of mail.

Luigi. Oh, yes, the uncle in the secret service, amateur scholar — hoy, there! L. L., of course. Kintyre felt chagrined. So much for that mystery. Bruce had only been noting those sections where he would be making an acknowledgment of his uncle's help.

Kintyre began leafing through. No point in reading every word about Aunt Sofia's arthritis or Cousin Giovanni's marriage. But there were pages, where Luigi described exactly what he had looked into for Bruce, that had not yet been transcribed. Those should be preserved, they were essential to the completion of the thesis.

Nothing else had occurred to Kintyre than that it would be finished and published, under Bruce's name.

Yes. Here was that reference to the Milanese archives. It concluded: "...would like to look through the libraries and store-rooms of the older aristocratic homes in this neighborhood. Quite possibly a contemporary reference exists, in a letter or diary. But the time and the introductions are not available to a poor policeman. Why do you not ask your rich American friend Clayton to have it done?"

Bruce's reply was grateful, but forebore to answer that faintly sarcastic question. Uncle Luigi took it up next time. Kintyre remembered the man, how he tried hard to be fair but was unable to refrain from cracks about Americans. It was only natural, if you were the patriot of a poor country: a form of self-defense.

"...Not another Medici. Do you seriously believe he cares about these old books? It is his particular camouflage, to get him among people of breeding who can be useful. His real friends are a coarser sort, if indeed he has any friends except his bank accounts."

Bruce protested: "...He had to make his own way in a world of fists. I think he has done very well, not only as a financier but as a human being. You cannot safely compare him with your own postwar newly-rich. From what I hear, many of them are crasser than any American parvenu ever dared to be. But let us not exchange ritual insults."

Uncle Luigi answered a query about the Sicilian terrain and twisted it around to his particular obsession: "...if you believe his standardized success story. Use your reason, my nephew. Clayton was an Army officer in this country during the last two years of the war. After his discharge, he came right back here. It is uncertain what he did in the next couple of years. Out of a slightly malicious curiosity I checked with the appropriate bureau, and he was registered only as a visitor, who went in and out of our borders. Then suddenly, in 1949, he applied for his business permits. He had obtained the American agency for that new line of motor scooters. Since then, his rise has been somewhat swifter than can be accounted for merely by pyramiding profits. What follows from this, Bruce? (And again I ask why your father had to become so American that he visited that name upon you.) Why, since he had only his military pay during the war, and on his civilian return had no source of income within Italy for two years — he must have been drawing on a considerable capital in America! Our records show him obtaining most of his lire for Swiss francs. Evidently he deposits his dollars in Switzerland, which you know has a free money market, converts them to other currencies as needed, buys goods, and ships those to America to earn more dollars. Therefore all this story he has told you (what is your phrase, from rags to Algernon?) is so much pretentious hokum. Clayton started as a rich man."

Margery came in with coffee. "What are you finding out?" she asked.

"Mostly gossip," said Kintyre. He repeated the gist to her.

"Oh, I remember that. It was several months ago." She sat down on the couch beside him. "Bruce was furious. He thought the world of Clayton. He wrote to Indianapolis and Des Moines and so on. It took him weeks to check everything, through local newspaper offices, old friends, that kind of reference. It's perfectly true, though. I doubt if Clayton had a thousand dollars left to his name when he joined the Army.

"Bruce hadn't gotten around to it yet, but he was going to assemble the facts, with clippings and personal correspondence, and send it all to Luigi in one devastating package. Especially after the last couple of letters he got. Luigi said there was no evidence Clayton had floated a loan to get his start, and wondered if he mightn't have done some currency black marketing. Bruce really blew his top at that."

"Oh?" said Kintyre. He should be on his way soon, he thought, and use the short time until then to be good to Margery. But a certain sense of the chase was on him. Trained to scan reading matter, he found the passage he wanted in a few minutes. Bruce's anger spoke through a cage of civilized words:

"...I am not one of our radical rightists, but I too resent this eternal meddling which is the modern idea of government. It would not surprise me if Clayton profited originally on the free exchange, when the postwar official rates were so ludicrously unreal. Who didn't, in those days? But if so, I say he did you all a service! I swear you could double your production over there simply by abolishing those medieval frontiers and restrictions, and putting the customs men to useful jobs!"

Luigi, after the inevitable reference to American tariffs, wrote: "The problem is more serious and urgent than you understand. One hears less about it than about your similar troubles, but we in the old countries are having our own postwar crime wave. And some of these syndicates are — not mere black markets, not mere smugglers of an occasional perfume bottle — but dealers in narcotics, prostitution, gun-running, extortion, blackmail, counterfeiting, corruption, and murder.

"Yes, I blame your government in part. We watch the criminals they deport to us, but we cannot forbid everyone to come talk to them. There is influence, there is advice. From the Communists these syndicates have also learned much, including the cell type of organization. We can arrest a man here and a man there, but he can only lead us to a few others. Sometimes we think we have identified an organizing brain, but it does not always follow that he can be seized. Not even in this country, where the police have a latitude that I am sure your Anglo-Saxon mind would be shocked by. I name no names, but now and again something rises to the surface, a scandal, the corpse of a young woman who belonged to a proud family, a member of the parliament seen in dubious places — and nothing comes of it. The newspapers are forbidden to follow the story to its end; everywhere protecting hands are reached out.

"Give us time, we will settle with these latter-day *condottieri*. Meanwhile, I could wish your Clayton were more circumspect in his choice of friends. He associates somewhat (not very much, to be sure, and there are business reasons) with a dealer named Dolce. And Dolce is a hard man from the slums of Naples. One of *his* associates is the deported Italian-American criminal chief named — "

Bruce's reply to this was a single explosive line: "And you used to wring your hands at me about Senator McCarthy!"

Kintyre put the box aside. He had been translating as he read, in a rapid mutter. "That's the end," he said. "Bruce wrote that two weeks ago, and I guess the uncle hasn't replied yet."

"Clayton," said Margery on a note of horror. "Do you think maybe — ?"

"That he's a crook? No. I don't know much about it, but I should certainly imagine that anybody who wanted to keep an import license would have to keep his nose pretty clean. If Clayton started hanging around with, oh, say Chicago gunmen, the FBI would be on his tail in a matter of weeks."

"But couldn't he — "

"Forget Clayton. He's alibied for every minute of that weekend. As for hiring professionals, look, pony, suppose you wanted such a job done. How would you find the pros?"

"Why — " She hesitated, lifting a small hand to her chin. "I don't know."

"You're a law-abiding citizen, so you don't know. Clayton is also reasonably law-abiding. He's got to be. The Italian police might conceivably not be aware of it if Clayton were doing something illicit. Over there, he could operate internationally. But the United States is another proposition. We talk about our free enterprise, but the plain fact is that an American business-man is required to operate in a goldfish bowl, under innumerable petti-fogging regulations. So,

I repeat, Clayton must be more or less straight. Even if the US government was unable to indict him for anything, they could rescind his various licenses, virtually by fiat.

"How, then, would he get in touch with an assassin? Walk into a tough bar and ask? Large laugh." Kintyre threw away his cigarette stub. "Oh, sure, given enough time, you or I or anyone could locate a murderer. But this job must have been done on short notice. There was nothing in Bruce's previous life to bring it on. You know how burblesome he was; could he have kept from you, for weeks, the fact that he knew something big? Of course not. Nor from me, or any of his associates. Ergo, it was something he blundered onto lately, probably without even realizing its significance. The person who was threatened by this had to react fast: find his killers and get them here, or do the job himself, within days. That lets Clayton out."

Margery nodded, a trifle overwhelmed. "I'm glad," she said. "I like him, the little I've seen."

"Yeh." Kintyre thought a couple of hours back. "Me too."

She smiled. "But there's still something that he isn't telling. I'm curious to know what."

"You may have your chance to find out tonight," said Kintyre. "I saw him and he mentioned he would call up and ask for a dinner date."

"Oh!" She looked at him, round-eyed. "And I haven't been answering!"

Kintyre laughed. "Turn up that phone bell right away, gal."

She shook her head. The blue eyes darkened with pain. "Only so I could say no in a nice way."

"Huh?"

"I'm not interested. Not yet." For an instant, there was a brightening across her face. "Unless you, Bob — "

"Sorry, kid. I'm tied up tonight." He checked his watch. "In fact, I should have left already."

"Oh," she said listlessly.

"Look here," he said. He took her by the shoulders and forced her to turn around and meet his gaze. "This can only go on so long, then they put you in the foundry. Bruce is dead. We're still alive. Start acting like it."

"It's only been — two days? Three?" She twisted away from him. "Give me time to get used to it."

"You never will, at this rate. I know you."

"You should," she said with a flick of anger. "Your castoff mistress."

"Castoff, hellfire! We terminated an association which — "

"Yes, yes. I've heard that line too. You warned me and so on. Go ahead, call yourself a gentleman."

"*Maròn!*" He sprang to his feet and paced the floor. She leaned back and watched him, breathing hard.

Eventually his temper cooled. "Margery," he said, "I think I know what Bruce meant to you. Besides being someone you cared for, I mean. He was your chance at emotional security, wasn't he? A home, children. Why don't you admit it, you'll always be the little girl from Ohio, and what's wrong with that? The average man will breed the unaverage one again, someday when the human race gets back its health. He has before. But these hipster types are a biological and cultural dead end.

"I can't build your house in Ohio for you. Forget me. Bruce was not your last chance, but if you sit on your tocus feeling sorry for yourself, he will have been. Get the devil out of this hole!"

"Thanks for the counsel," she said. It fell flatly on his ears. The rising fury tinted her and tensed her; she spoke through jaws held stiff. "So much cheaper than help, isn't it? But it happens I choose to stay home tonight. Alone. Starting at once."

Kintyre stopped in midstride. "I'm sorry," he said. "I'm not sure what I did wrong just now, but I'm sorry."

She slumped. "Please go away," she said without tone. "Call me tomorrow if you want, but please go away now."

"All right," he said.

She didn't stir as he went out the door.

He walked fast, being late. Anger changed to concern, and then that faded too, when he had Corinna to think about. Margery would be feeling better tomorrow, he could make friends again. At the moment, he needed a bath and a shave and a change of clothes.

Headlines on a news rack caught his eye, an extra edition. Peter and Eugene Michaelis had been arrested on suspicion of murder.

12

Corinna had an apartment on a quiet street not far from Golden Gate Park. Kintyre had been told by Bruce that she worked on the staff of a small art museum, belonged to a little theater group, owned a light target rifle, and made most of her own clothes. He had seen for himself that she spoke Italian. That was all. He felt ridiculously like a schoolboy on his first date.

She opened her door and smiled him in. High heels put her almost on a level with him. She wore black, which set off her pale hair, but the sleeves flared and the skirt swirled: it was not mourning.

"I'm nearly ready, Dr. Kintyre. Won't you sit down? Watch out for the cat, she bites."

Kintyre enjoyed cats; he would have kept one himself if he had wanted to assume obligations. This was that loveliest of the tribe, a blue-point Siamese, white as new snow and markings like twilight. She flowed up toward his extended fist as he settled in a chair. "What's the name?" he asked.

"Taffimai Metallumai," said Corinna, returning to her bedroom. "If you remember your Kipling, that means Small-Person-Without-Any-Manners-Who-Ought-To-Be-Spanked. But she lives under the name of Tipsy. Gold letters over her door, and so on."

He looked around. This room was individualistically decorated, she must have done it herself, in reds and blues and a couple of delicate Chinese paintings. Her books ran toward poetry, drama, and art; but one shelf held the popular works of Gamow, Russell, Ley, and company. There was a medium-fi and a lot of good records.

Taffimai Metallumai levitated up onto his lap, gave him a sleepy turquoise look, and ordered him to scratch her beneath the chin. She was pure hard muscle under the virginal fur; she must weigh twice as much as any peasant cat her size.

Kintyre took his attention from the corner where a small worktable held an unfinished papier-mâché mask. Corinna was coming back in. "That was quick," he said, rising.

"Oh, don't! You're catted! Oh, dear!"

He looked at his gashed thumb. Tipsy told him in a few well chosen words that he had no business upsetting her without warning.

Corinna's eyes were green distress. "People never do believe my warning," she said, "and then Snow Leopard j.g. makes a lunch off them and — Can I tell you how sorry I am?"

"Occupational hazard if you like cats," Kintyre answered. "And I do. We might put on some stickum, just for appearances."

She regarded him closely. "I believe you mean that," she said. "Thank you." She led him to the bathroom. The route gave him a glimpse of her kitchen and a crammed shelf of herbs and spices.

"Instead of going out," he said as he repaired the damage, "I could probably get a better dinner here."

"Why, I hadn't prepared anything, but — "

"Nonsense. Maybe you'll give me a rain check. Let's go."

Tipsy assured him that she bore no hard feelings, and he stroked her with real pleasure. It occurred to him that there was something pathetic about Margery's little caged parakeet, set beside this beautiful killing engine.

"You're quite a scientist," he remarked, nodding at the books.

"Only as a spectator," said Corinna. "I would have liked to get a degree in math, but we hadn't the money and I was needed to help in the restaurant." Her explanation was unresentful.

He helped her into her coat and they went down to his car. "Where are we going?" she asked.

"I know a Dutch place near Russian Hill," he told her. "Ever been there? No? Good. Dutch cuisine is badly underrated. It's fully comparable to the French, in its own way."

She fell silent. He stole a look at the Egyptian profile; it was grave again.

"Forgive me if I'm tactless," he said.

"You aren't. You're very kind to come and — What good would we do Bruce, sitting around with our faces dragging on the floor?"

"I thought as much myself," he ventured. "But then, I was only a friend."

"Bruce never had a better one. I rather imagine you knew him more intimately than any of his kin. He grew away from us, toward something of his own. As was right, of course."

Kintyre had no reply.

"And then," she said in a matter-of-fact tone, "he was good. Not holy, but good. I don't think he will be too long in Purgatory."

Kintyre, for whom the soul was a metaphor, had to think over every aspect of her remark until he could understand that, quite simply, she believed it. That was not a consolation he wished to take from her.

"But damn," she whispered, "I'll miss him!"

They drove on in silence. At last she said, more awkwardly than the average modern woman: "I have to ask you about one thing. I saw a newspaper today. This girl he — he knew — "

"Yes," said Kintyre, focusing intently on the traffic. "I know her. They were living together. She's an altogether fine person who would have made him a wonderful wife. Bruce was very much in love with her and wanted to get married. She hesitated only because she — was afraid she might hurt him — she would have changed her mind soon. They were happy."

Corinna sighed. He could almost feel how she relaxed. "Thank you," she said. "I have a lot to thank you for, haven't I? We needn't say any more about this except — if the girl would like to see me, or have me visit her, I'd be more than glad to."

"I think so," said Kintyre. "In a few more days."

At once he damned himself for an idiot. He had spoken truth; but it gave Margery the chance to relate a few truths of her own, if she chose, and what might come of that?

They spoke little for the remainder of the drive. It was, somehow, a restful quietness.

It was broken when they stepped from the car. Another news rack faced them, with ARREST FATHER, SON FOR LOMBARDI MURDER staggering across the page.

Corinna drew a gasp. She snatched Kintyre's hand with fingers that were suddenly cold. "*Santa Maria*," she mumbled.

He steadied her. "Easy, there," he said.

"I knew it." Her voice came saw-toothed. "I knew it was them. What does it say?"

He bent over the page. "Not much more than that. Picked up this afternoon on suspicion, father and son. No details."

"It'll be out tomorrow. Everything. And then the trial."

"I thought you were all for this," he said. "You were convinced of their guilt and — "

"I wasn't thinking. I was only hurt, and tired. No, I don't want it to be this way." Slowly, she stiffened herself. "But so be it, then. Can I have a drink?"

"You can have more than that." He steered her along the sidewalk. She still moved a little unsurely. "You can have the news I mainly came to give you."

"What?"

"The Michaelises are not guilty."

A bar stood by their path. He led her inside, to a booth. The drab routine of checking Corinna's age seemed to help calm her. She asked for straight Irish whisky, he took beer.

Only then did she challenge him: "How do you know?"

"It's a long story," he said, "and frankly, I'm not certain how much of it you should hear. So suppose you begin by telling me why you think they did it."

"The police — "

"Uh-huh. They paid a little more attention to your ideas than you thought. They checked and found Gene had dropped out of sight over the weekend. He and his father refused to cooperate, doubtless being very surly about it, so now they're in the calaboose. But what could their motive have been in the first place?"

Her fingers twisted together. "Oh, all that business years ago, when their boat rammed Dad's."

"What more? It's something to do with you, isn't it?"

"Yes. Nothing disgraceful, I suppose. But ugly. A million people sniggering over this new revelation about our family — isn't there going to be end to it, ever?"

The drinks came. She tossed hers off recklessly and asked for another. While she waited, and he worked on his beer, she looked squarely across the table at him and said:

"Gene came back from the Navy last summer. He looked up Bruce in Berkeley. Bruce took him home to our parents for dinner; I happened to be there too. Gene gave me quite a play. He could be very charming. We had a number of dates." The color crept into her face, but she went on: "Yes, he did his best to seduce me. When that didn't work, he asked me to marry him. Every time we went out, it would end up with a proposal — and a wrestling match. I liked him, though. And he'd moved back to San Francisco from the Eastbay, taken a different job, just to be near me. Who wouldn't be flattered, and touched? But I finally had to lay down the law. It was a fight, physically, to make him behave. I caught a taxi home."

The waitress came back. Corinna picked up her second glass and sipped slowly. "He apologized the next day," she said, "but I told him I couldn't go out with him any more. He seemed to take it pretty well, said he would go back to Chicago — he'd spent a lot of time there once — but he asked for some kind of send-off. I — I spoke to Bruce. Gene had always been an admirer of Bruce. Odd, that big, husky, world-tramping fellow, admiring Bruce. We couldn't just drop him like that. We arranged a double date for a weekend early in December, a trip down to Carmel. I knew Bruce was in love, he couldn't hide that, but I asked him to take a friend of mine from the theater. It would make the atmosphere different. Safer, I thought."

Corinna stared into her drink. "We got a couple of hotel rooms down there," she said flatly. "We did a little drinking. Gene did more than a little. He made several open passes at me. I was afraid of a fight, but this girl and I got to bed at last. Back in their room, Gene's and Bruce's, Gene kept on drinking. He urged Bruce to come with him, into our room. Well, what would you expect? Bruce lost his temper and threw a punch at him. It couldn't have hurt — outside — but I wonder what it did to Gene, really. He started screaming about how we were all against him. I could hear him through the wall. We'd come down in his car. He said we could all find our own way home, he staggered out to his car and drove back along the highway — drunk."

Corinna brought her voice under control again. "That's all. We heard of the accident after we got home next day on the bus. We went to see him in the hospital as soon as we could. How he cursed us! Bruce was crying too, when we left."

"I know," said Kintyre. "I saw him a day or so later." And, briefly, he told her what Margery had done.

She seemed to thaw before his eyes. "If there could be such a thing as a blessed sin — "

"Now let's return to business," said Kintyre. "I want to get the nightmare off your back. *Imprimis*, how sorry are you for Gene? Actually?"

She hesitated. At last: "That's impossible to answer."

"He got what he asked for. It's pure luck the man in the other car wasn't killed."

"I suppose so." Hardness grew along her jawline. "And if he murdered my brother — how does the saying go? God may forgive him, but I never can."

"Good. However, *secundus*: He was not involved in Bruce's death."

"What makes you so certain?" she demanded, almost belligerently.

"Let me tell you what happened last night." *Was it only last night?*

He related it in a few words. She looked at him so strangely that he was puzzled, until it came to him that not many college professors enter waterfront tenements and throw people around.

"I hope you don't think I asked for the brawl," he finished. "I'm ashamed of it. But it gave me the proof I needed."

Her hand stole out, toward the plaster on his forehead. "Is that how you got hurt?" she asked softly.

"No." He continued hastily: "A strong possibility is that Bruce was killed by professionals. Imported murderers are likeliest, since the police will be seining all local toughs."

"Gene lived in Chicago," she murmured through tightened lips.

"Gene and his father are stonkering poor. Even if Gene has a murderer friend, such a job would not be done just as a favor."

"Then they could have done it themselves, father and son."

"Look, we had a minor scrap, the three of us. Those walls are like paper. Half the building heard it and came pounding on the door. Bruce could not have been — hurt, as he was — in that place. It would have to be somewhere else. Consider all the practical difficulties, finding an abandoned warehouse or whatever. Getting an automobile, for heaven's sake! Where would paupers like those two find the money to rent a car, even for a day?

"Oh, well, if we stretch our reasoning all out of shape, we can say they *might* have done all that. But one thing they could never have managed, and that was to capture Bruce in the first place. He would have tied them in bowknots."

"Bruce?" She was openly bewildered.

"Yes. Stop thinking of him as a mere bookworm. Bruce and I were going to pack into Kings Canyon, which is still pretty wild. And he was taking up judo, and doing quite well. A gun could have taken him prisoner, of course, but the Michaelises don't have a gun; they'd have gone for it last night if one were on the premises. So Bruce would have had to be slugged from behind. But there was no mark of a club on his body, no anesthetic — I have that from the police. Weaponless, neither Gene nor his father could have held Bruce for ten seconds. They're both strong, but they fall over themselves. I threw them with baby techniques."

"That's right," she said, "you do go in for judo, don't you? But Bruce said you were an expert."

"I only wear a brown belt so far. Bruce, of course, was a white. He could not have coped with one or two men who knew how to handle themselves — not necessarily judo men, just experienced fighters." *Consider Terry Larkin.* "However, he could certainly have thrown two unarmed Michaelises. Take my word for it. I know."

"Oh."

She studied her hands for a while.

"They'll be released in a few days at the outside," said Kintyre. "The most elementary procedures will show they're innocent. I can think of a dozen lines of proof myself. To be sure, you may be subjected to some publicity before that happens, but it will never get as far as a grand jury. Believe me."

"Thank you." When she smiled, he could see no other thing in all that dingy building. "I always seem to be thanking you."

"Which I find pleasant enough," he bowed.

"Why don't we go down to the station and explain it right now?" she asked hesitantly. "You're not afraid of being arrested for the fight, are you? That wasn't your fault."

"Oh, no. But my testimony and my reasoning aren't legally conclusive," he evaded.

"It would help a lot. It might get them out, tip the scales. I feel so sorry for them now. That poor old man!"

Kintyre looked straight into the green eyes. "Will you trust me a little bit?" he said. "Will you take my word that we can't do it immediately?"

Because the police would inquire further. Did I indeed hurt my arm and my head in that fracas? No, say the Michaelises. Where, then? I do not think their search would end short of Guido, your brother.

She bit her lip. "I hate to think of them locked up for something they haven't done."

"At the present time," he said, "my story would compromise someone else whom I also know to be innocent."

Like hell I do.

She sighed. "All right. That's good enough for me." And then, with the morning of her smile upon him again: "You've done enough for one day's knight errantry. Let's go eat."

13

The restaurant was small and quiet. Corinna and Kintyre had a corner table, where the light fell gently.

"By rights we should have a Genever apéritif," he said, "but I'm convinced Dutch gin is distilled from frogs. On the other hand, Dutch beer compares to Hof, Rothausbräu, or Kronenbourg."

"You've traveled a lot, haven't you?" she said. "I envy you that. Never got farther than the Sierras myself."

A little embarrassed — he had not been trying to play the cosmopolite — he fell silent while she glanced at her menu. "Will you order for me?" she asked finally. "You know your way around these dishes."

He made his selections, pleased by the compliment. When the beer came, in conical half-liter glasses, he raised his: *"Prosit."*

"Salute." She drank slowly. "Wonderful. But this may not be wise on top of two whiskies."

"It's all right if you go easy. Take the word of a hardened bowser." He searched out an inward weariness on the strong broad face. "You could use a little anesthesia."

"Well — " She set her glass down. "Bear with me. I promise not to blubber, but I may get sentimental. Or maybe even hilarious, I don't know. I've never lost anyone close to me before now."

"I understand," said Kintyre.

"And please help me steer clear of myself," she added. "I would like to talk about Bruce, and otherwise about wholly neutral things." She managed a smile. "I've been meaning to ask you something. You're the Machiavelli specialist. Our theater did *Mandragola* last year. Tell me, how could the same man write that and *Il Principe*?"

"Actually," said Kintyre, "I would be surprised if the author of *The Prince* — or, rather, the *Discourses on Livy*, since *The Prince* is really just a pamphlet — I'd be surprised if he had not done sheer amusement equally well. One of the more damnable heresies of this era is its notion that a man can only be good at one thing. That versatility is not the inborn human norm."

"I've often thought the same," she said. "I suppose you know Bruce changed his major to history because of you. He took one of your classes as a freshman. Now I see why."

"Well," he stalled, and hoisted his beer.

She shifted the conversation with a tact he appreciated: "But how did you happen to get interested in it, in the Italian Renaissance yet, with a name like yours?"

"I served time in one of those private schools back East," he said. "The Romance languages master got me enthusiastic."

He paused, then continued slowly: "I entered Harvard, but Pearl Harbor happened in my sophomore year. I was in the Navy the whole war, the Pacific; fell in love with the Bay Area on my shore leaves, which is why I came here to live afterward. But during the war I had a lot of time to read and try to think where this world was going. To the wolves, I decided — like Machiavelli's world — I suppose that's why I feel so close to him. He was also studying the problem of how the decent man can survive. He spoke the truth as he saw it, because he didn't think that civilization should be encumbered with nice-nellyisms that the barbarians had already discarded. Wherefore he became the original Old Nick, and the very people — us, the free people, whom he could warn — won't listen, because we think he speaks for the enemy!"

He braked. "Sorry. I didn't mean to orate at you."

"I wish more men had convictions," she said. "Even when I don't agree. Everybody respects everybody else's sensibilities so much these days, there's nothing left to talk about but football scores."

"You're very kind," he said. "Ah, here come the appetizers. Pay special attention to the characteristically Dutch delicacy, Russian eggs, but don't ask me how they came by that name."

Later, after much talk, some of it with enough laughter to tell him she was a merry soul in better days:

A ruby spark lay in their glasses of Cherry Heering. "This isn't Dutch either," said Kintyre. "However."

"Do you know," she said, "I begin to understand the old idea of a wake. Getting the clan together and having one fine brawling celebration. It's more an act of love, really, than drawing the parlor curtains and talking in hushed voices."

"That's the Latin who speaks," he said. "We Protestant races are cursed with the tradition that misery is a virtue."

"But you, you Bostonian Scot or whatever you are — I hear a trace of accent — *you* approve."

"I left Boston for the Pacific at the arthritic age of nine."

"What was the reason for that?"

"My father was a marine architect. He was laid off in, uh, 1930. Being an imaginative man, he spent his savings on a schooner, hired a Mexican crew, and we all lit out for the South Seas. For seven years we lived on that schooner."

"Bruce told me you were a sailor." Her eyes were very bright upon him. "But how did you make it pay?"

"Miscellaneously. Sometimes we carried cargo and passengers between islands. The passengers were usually Kanakas, and those who didn't have money would pay us in food and hospitality when we got where we were going. Father wasn't after riches anyway. His main enterprise was to gather and prepare marine specimens, for museums and colleges and so on. Toward the end, he was making a name for himself. Well, we never saw much cash money, but we never needed a lot either."

Kintyre held his glass to the light, tossed it off and followed it with a scalding sip of coffee. Why was he speaking of this? He had barely mentioned his youth to anyone else, except Trig, who was the friend of a dozen years. Trig had led him into the dojo, hoping that its discipline of mind as well as body would strangle the horror. But Corinna had the story out of him in a matter of hours, not even knowing what she did.

He had taken her for Morna last night.

"What happened?" she asked. Her tone said that he needn't answer unless he wanted to.

"A typhoon and a lee shore," he said. "I was the only survivor."

He took out a cigarette. She folded her hands and waited, in case he should want to say more.

"That was in the Gilbert Islands," he continued after the smoke was curling down his tongue. "The British authorities shipped me home. The guardianship was wished onto a cousin of my mother's. So I went to the boarding school I spoke of, and summers I worked at a seaside resort. Don't feel sorry for me, it was quite a good life."

"But a lonely one," she said.

He grinned with a single corner of his mouth. "'*He travels the fastest who travels alone.*'"

"I understand a great deal now." She held her cup so lightly that he grew aware he was in danger of breaking his. Tendon by tendon, he eased his fingers. "Yes," she said after a moment. "Bruce was always puzzled by you. As I imagine most people are. You don't seem to belong anywhere, to anything or anyone. And yet you do. You belong to a world that foundered in the ocean."

It jarred him. Not given to self-analysis, he had imagined he lived a logical, well adapted round of days.

"Sometime you'll build it again," she said. "Oh, not the physical ship, you've more important things on hand, but a personal world."

And again it was a blow, to be shown himself as alien as a castaway from Mars.

"Please," he said, more roughly than he had intended. "I don't find my personality the most interesting object on earth."

She nodded, as if to herself. The long hair swept her flat high-boned cheeks. "Of course. You wouldn't."

"Perhaps I'd better take you home now," he said, without noticeable enthusiasm. "Are you working tomorrow?"

"Only if I feel like it, my boss told me. I'd planned to, but — Are you in any hurry?"

"Contrariwise." *I don't think I would sleep much.*

"Then could we go somewhere and talk? I'd like to ask you some things."

"I'd love to be asked. I know a place."

It was small, dark, and masculine, undegraded by jukebox or television. Kintyre led Corinna into a booth at the rear.

"They serve steam beer," he said. "The only really good beer made in this country."

"Oof! I couldn't. Another Irish, if I may. I promise to go slow." Her tone was not as light as the words.

Nonetheless, he needed a little while to sense the trouble in her.

After much time she met his eyes, obviously forcing his own. "Dr. Kintyre," she began.

He was about to ask her to use his given name; and then he thought how little intimacy could be achieved in this American cult of first-name familiarity with all the universe. "Yes?" he said.

"I would — I would have thanked you for a wonderful time, which helped me more than you know. And then I would have gone home. But — "

He waited.

"I don't know how to say it," she stumbled. "I knew you were Bruce's — Bruce's brother, the one he should have had. But only tonight could I *feel* it." She searched for a phrase. Finally: "I don't believe I could hurt myself by being serious with you."

"I hope not," he said, as grave as she. "I can't promise it."

"Why did you go to the Michaelises last night?"

"I'm not quite sure."

"You want to discover who killed Bruce? Isn't that it?"

"I am not a self-appointed detective. The police can do that job infinitely better than I. But I have been thinking."

"What do you think?" she persisted.

"I certainly wouldn't go accusing someone who — "

"Can you realize what Bruce meant to me?" She asked it quietly, as a meaningful request for truth. "We were more than siblings. We were friends, all our lives, in a way they haven't made words for."

"I do know," he said, and he would have told it to few other creatures that lived. "I had a younger sister myself."

"Even after he left home — can you imagine the way he continued to watch over me? How often he stepped in and used a word or two to straighten out a lonesome, confused, unhappy girl whom nobody else liked; how he steered me toward the kind of people I can feel at home with; how he healed the breach with my parents, when I *had* to get away and they didn't understand; how he got me out of a wretched business office and into the museum, where I can like what I'm doing and believe it has some value. You knew Bruce, did you know that side of him?"

"No," said Kintyre. "He wouldn't have talked about it. Still, yes, I can imagine."

"And he was lured somewhere, and tortured, and murdered," she said. The lacquered fingernails stood white where she caught the table edge.

Kintyre didn't touch her himself, but he held out his hand. She gripped it for a while. Her face was lowered. When she let go and looked up again, he saw tears.

"I'm sorry," she gulped. "I promised not to bawl, and then — "

Kintyre let her have it out. It didn't take long, nor was it noisy.

She said at last, in a wire-thin voice: "Why was it done? Who would do it, to him of all people in the world?"

"I don't know," said Kintyre. "I just don't know."

"But you can guess, can't you? You know everyone concerned. That writer he was having the fight with. That businessman who owns the thesis manuscript. Gene Michaelis. You could be wrong! Even his girl, God help me for saying it. Who?"

"Why must you know?" he asked.

"Why?" It took her aback. "To know! To understand —"

"Do you want to be reassured the murderer won't strike at you next? I hardly think you need fear that."

"Of course not!" she flared. "I want to know so the world can make some sense again."

"That's too metaphysical to be true," he said.

Briefly, she shivered with tension. Then, leaning back, she picked up her whisky glass and sipped of it and asked coldly:

"Where did you go last night after you left the Michaelis place?"

"Home," he said.

"Guido was badly shaken today. He hadn't slept at all, I could see that in the morning. He stayed around the apartment like a hurt animal. I know him, he's terrified." Corinna spat as if at an enemy: "What did you do to him?"

"Nothing!" said Kintyre.

Her lip caught her teeth.

"I didn't think of it till just now," she breathed. "But it all fits. You do know something. In God's name, tell me!"

He said, with an overpowering compassion: "I see. You're afraid Guido is involved."

"Yes," she said dully.

"Why should he be?"

"Oh — I don't know — jealousy? Who can tell? Guido always seemed like the wild, reckless one and Bruce a mama's boy. Yet it was Bruce who left home and Guido never has."

"Let's have no half-digested psychological theory," he said, purposely astringent. "Stick to facts. What leads you to suspect your brother is involved?"

"I might as well tell you," she sighed. "Last week he was dropping all kinds of dark hints about a big job which would take him out of town over the weekend. He's like that, has to sound important, mostly there's no harm in it. But he came back Monday evening with a good deal of money. I knew he was broke before. He had even been forced to sell his car. He came in loaded with expensive presents for all of us, and had a fat roll in his wallet. Of course, when we told him about Bruce, that more or less made us forget it. But then today, how frightened he was —"

"What happened last night?"

Kintyre took out a cigarette. "Excuse me while I think," he said. He made a ceremony of lighting it.

"Guido is in trouble," he admitted. "I don't know how closely related to the murder it is."

"Don't misunderstand me." Her face could have been modeled in chalk. "I never thought Guido would — would dream of — no! But he could have been drawn into something. And what would the police think?"

"Uh-huh. The same notion occurred to me."

"What happened, then?"

He told her.

"Oh, no." Her eyes closed.

"You see my dilemma," he said wearily. "I'll protect Guido if my conscience will let me, even though it's already led me into lawbreaking. But I don't know, I can't tell —"

She opened her eyes again. They blazed.

"Thank You," she said, not to Kintyre.

His scalp crawled. "What are you thinking of?"

"I know Guido," she answered. "I can get the truth out of him."

"You can try."

She stood up. "I'll take a cab," she said.

"What?" He rose himself. "You're not going there now?"

"When else? I'm sorry, it's a shabby way to treat you, but do you think something like this can wait?"

"A murderer is hanging around that place," he said. "You can see Guido tomorrow at your parents', but tonight I won't have it."

She grinned. There was even a little humor in the expression. "What do you plan to do?"

"Call the police!" he rapped.

She said like a sword: "By the time you've explained all the ins and outs to them, I'll have taken him elsewhere. And you needn't bother speaking to either of us again."

He took her by the wrist. "Let me go," she said, almost casually.

"Wait a second." Again he knew the night feeling, that he must go, and that that would happen which another force than he had willed. But somehow, crazily, this time he was glad of it.

"Just wait for me," he finished.

14

The doorkeeper-bouncer was the first obstacle. Kintyre wished he had worn a hat. Nothing disguised him except a gray suit; the square of bandage at his hairline felt like a searchlight.

"Follow my lead," whispered Corinna as they went down the stairs.

It was dark in the doorway, and narrow. She contrived to get herself squeezed between Kintyre and the other man; and as she slithered by she threw him such a look that he would have let a rhinoceros enter unnoticed beside her.

The Alley Cat was full tonight. Mostly the cool crowd, Kintyre judged, drawn by the rumors of last night's affair. He could not help himself, but whispered to Corinna: "Where in the hell did you learn to put five thousand volts of raw sex into three motions and one sidelong glance?"

"Theater." Even at this moment, when she saw through a harsh blue haze her brother who might be a murderer singing a dirty ballad, she could have been a female Puck. "Also, it helps to live with a cat."

They threaded their way along the wall until they found a table in shadow. "We can see him at the intermission," he proposed. She nodded. The waitress who lit their candle — Kintyre snuffed it again when she had left — and brought them a demi of burgundy, paid them no special attention. Well, it was long established that an excited eyewitness has no value. Those who saw the fight had not really seen the fighters.

Corinna fell silent, resting her cheek on one fist. She didn't drink at all. Kintyre tried to read the way she was looking at Guido, but understood only a troubled tenderness.

"Mind if I join you?"

Kintyre looked up, startled, into Trygve Yamamura's flat face. "Oh," he said stupidly. "Sit down. Miss Lombardi, this is — " He explained in detail.

"I'm glad to know you," she said. Her eyes added: *Maybe. It will depend on what comes next.* Guido's guitar twanged and capered. His voice overrode the room, as full of satyr laughter as if it had never known anything else. "With his whack-fol-de-diddle-di-day — "

"Were we that conspicuous coming in?" whispered Kintyre.

"Lay off the stage hiss," Yamamura told him. "A low speaking voice draws less attention. No, you pulled it off okay. It was only that I was making it my business to see everyone who comes in. Still am." His eyes remained in motion as he sat holding his beer; the rest of him was nearly limp, taking its ease until a muscle should be needed.

"Been here long?" asked Kintyre.

"Couple hours, since the act went on," said Yamamura. "I tailed Guido from his place. Before then, though, I assumed he wouldn't leave his four safe walls, so I found plenty to do elsewhere."

Corinna exclaimed: "You learned something?"

"Uh-huh. I came right over this morning after Bob saw me. No grass grows where I have been, I mean no grass grows under my feet." Yamamura took a pipe from his maroon sports jacket. "The best way to get a line on your friend Larkin seemed to be to check Guido's recent movements. I started at the other end — his call on Clayton, a week ago last Monday. You know, when he and Bruce went around to see about a job. Clayton himself isn't in the City today, but I went to that swank apartment hotel he inhabits and jollied the staff."

Having filled his pipe, he took his time lighting it. "I gather Clayton gave Guido and Bruce a rather long interview," he went on. "Or, rather, Bruce. Guido left about an hour before his brother did."

"He never mentioned that!" said Corinna.

"Why should he?" countered Yamamura. "Not good for his pride, is it? But what did Bruce and Clayton find to talk about?"

"And how much of it did Guido hear?" murmured Kintyre.

Corinna flushed. "Please don't," she said in a hard voice.

"I'm sorry," he answered, torn. "But if Bruce had to tell Clayton something important, even worth killing about — they'd shoo Guido out first. But Guido might have gotten enough hints to make some deductions and — No, wait, let me finish! Maybe Guido blabbed to someone else, not realizing himself what it signified."

She gave him a shaky little smile. "Thanks for trying," she said.

"Ah, this is probably of no significance at all," said Yamamura. "Bruce could just as well have been giving Clayton the latest information about the mildew on page 77 of that book." He attempted a smoke ring and failed. "Or could he? Depends on how you interpret this tidbit: Clayton telephoned Genoa, Italy, that same night."

"Who did he call?" asked Kintyre.

"The switchboard girl doesn't remember. All she heard was a lot of Italian: they started gabbling right away, before she could take herself out of the circuit. Clayton stayed home for several hours next day. The Italian called again. Now none of this would be worth retailing, I guess, except for one more oddity about Mr. Clayton. He had the bellhop bring him several dollars in change. Then he went out and was gone for some hours."

Corinna raised her thick dark brows in puzzlement. Kintyre nodded. "Yes. Long-distance, though not transatlantic, calls from a public booth," he said. "No chance of being eavesdropped on."

"It may not mean a damn relevant thing," said Yamamura. "The most legitimate businesses have their secrets. But I'll admit to being curious. Did Bruce steer him onto something big? And did a business rival then strike at Bruce? That doesn't sound likely. Maybe Clayton himself — no, hardly that. In my line of work I'd have heard it if he weren't straight, or if he associated with thugs."

Kintyre jammed his fists into knots. An intake of air hissed between his teeth.

"What is it?" Corinna's alarm seemed to come from far away.

"Nothing. Or possibly something. Never mind. Go on, Trig."

Only part of him heard the detective continue. The rest said through thunder: *One more suspect. I had been sure Clayton, of all people, must be innocent. For the Federal government would have assured itself he knows no assassins — Trig, perhaps more reliably, tells me the same — and he could not have found any on short notice, and it is impossible he could have done the crime personally.*

But Guido might have such connections!

Did Clayton see Guido again?

"Then I went around and chivvied the cops," said Yamamura. "They were just hauling in the Michaelis family, and hadn't much time for any other ideas. However, they are going to check house rentals over the weekend. You see, what was done — I'm sorry, Miss Lombardi — the deed would require an isolated spot. An entire house, at least. For the noise."

"Has anything come of that?" asked Corinna with a great steadiness.

"Not yet. These things take time. Well, then I had some supper and came here. Wasn't open yet, but they were making ready. Someone will have to meet my expense account, twenty-five good dollars to grease my way in and learn something."

"I can," said Corinna.

"Not you, Miss Lombardi. Most especially not you." Yamamura fumbled with his pipe; he was all at once an unhappy man. "Must I say it?"

Her eyes closed again, a flicker of aloneness. Then: "Please. It's better now, isn't it, than later from someone else?"

"A couple of strangers were in here last Thursday night. They introduced themselves to Guido, stood him drinks, talked at length. All this was noticed by the bartender, without any special interest, simply because it was a slack midweek night. He didn't hear what was said. After closing time, Guido went out with them.

"The description of one of those birds answers moderately well to Bob's description of Larkin."

Corinna shook herself, as if something rode her neck. "Is that all?" she asked.

"Yes."

"It could be worse," she said. "We already know he knows Larkin."

"What did the other man look like?" asked Kintyre.

"Smallish fellow, sandy-haired, long nose. And I'm surprised the barkeep could tell me that much. Look how you've come right back in here tonight, a stranger, after tearing the joint up."

Guido finished. Applause crackled, abnormally loud for a place like this: did they clap the knife which had been drawn? wondered Kintyre.

Corinna got up and made her way toward the platform. Guido gaped at her. "I like that girl," said Yamamura. "Do we have to go on with this business?"

"If we don't, she will alone," Kintyre told him.

Corinna and Guido held a muted argument. The fear was bulging his eyes. Finally he collapsed, somehow, and went out through the rear door. Corinna followed.

"Here we go," said Yamamura. "No, you ape, don't blow your nose! Oldest trick in the book, and you can bet there's at least one plainclothesman here tonight."

He sauntered affably between the tables. Kintyre came behind, his shoulders aching with tension. The bartender, the man who could actually notice things, regarded him speculatively as he passed by. A small surf of conversation lapped at his feet, he had to choke down the idiotic belief that it was all about him.

Then they were in the back room. Kintyre recognized the alley door he had used previously. Almost hidden by stacked beer cases, a stair led upward. At its top they found a dusty room with an iron cot, a couple of chairs, and an old vanity table. A naked electric bulb glared from the ceiling. Dressing room, Kintyre supposed.

Guido sat on the bedstead. He held a cigarette to his lips and drew on it as if it kept him alive. Corinna stood before him. The overhead light made her hair into a helmet and her face into a mask. Shadows lay huge in the corners.

Guido didn't look up. "I'll see you later," he mumbled. "I swear it. But not here. For Chrissake, we can all be killed here."

"Then why did you come tonight?" asked Yamamura.

"God! I was afraid not to."

"Did you see anyone dangerous in the audience?"

"I can't tell." His forehead glistened under the tangled hair. "There's a baby spot on me when I sing. I can't see past the first couple tables."

Corinna said: "Mr. Yamamura is a private detective. I understand he's even better at judo than Dr. Kintyre, which you should know is saying quite a lot."

"And when they go home?" He lifted a skull face. "What happens to me then?"

Yamamura replied: "Your only real safety will come when those people you are afraid of have been settled with. Do you want to go the rest of your life being afraid?"

"You can't settle with them," whispered Guido. "I mean, it's not just Larkin with his switchblades. O'Hearn carries a gun, and he's a three-time loser already, do you understand what that means? I've seen his gun!"

"Is there anyone else?" asked Kintyre.

"I don't know. You expect me to tell you if I do? I'll get myself killed!"

Corinna waved Kintyre and Yamamura back. She sat down beside Guido and took his free hand. "Bruce got himself killed too," she said in her gentlest tone.

"Oh, yes, yes, yes! Leave me alone!"

"He was tied down somewhere and tortured," she said, not raising her voice. "They burned him. The marks were all over his body, even after they finished hacking it up. I know that much, no more. Nobody would tell me more, and I didn't want to ask. But he must have been glad when they finally cut his throat."

Guido tried to rise. She pulled him back, without using much strength. "Jesus!" he screamed.

"Why did you help them?" she asked.

"I didn't! It's got nothing to do with —I *didn't!*"

She stood up again and looked down upon him. "Why did you do it?" she said as calmly. "How had he hurt you, that you had to let him be burned and twisted and killed?"

"No! Not me! I don't know!" His mouth was stretched into a gash; a tongue like dry wood bobbed within it.

She slapped him. It could not have been hard, but he fell back onto the bed and clawed at the mattress.

"Good-by," she said, and walked from him.

Kintyre looked at her and knew why the Furies had been women. His heart was a cold lump.

Corinna waited in a corner, her hands writhing together. Guido tried, horribly, to weep, and could not.

Then at last he rolled over on his back, blinked at the light, and said in a high childish voice: "I'll tell you what happened. I'll tell you so you can see it wasn't me, wasn't anything to do with Bruce, it just happened to happen the same weekend, and then maybe if you get out and leave me alone they won't kill me.

"All I did was this. These cats from Chicago came around last week and said they were after some of the pod and could I get it, it was worth five hundred bucks to them plus expenses. Not horse, now, I don't have anything to do with horse. Just marijuana, it never hurt anybody, you don't get hooked, you don't go nuts, hell, I mean you even have to will yourself to keep the jag up and it's only in your head, man, you don't do nothing to nobody else, dig?"

"Guido," said Corinna warningly.

He snapped after air. Presently he continued: "So I told them I didn't handle it myself but I knew some who did. But they didn't dig that, said they didn't want nothing to do with any local pushers, they didn't even want it from any near town. Well, it seemed way out to me, but five hundred plus expenses for finding a small packet wasn't to be turned down, so I asked around and got the name of a dealer in Tijuana, and when I saw them the next day they said that would do. So I rented a car and drove down Saturday. I was supposed to meet Larkin here again Monday night and give him the packet and get the rest of my money — they paid two-fifty in advance. I came back to town late Monday. When I hit my pad I heard about Bruce and the old lady was crying all over me, so I called the place here and talked with Larkin, could he meet me Tuesday night instead. So he said all right, only the professor was here when he arrived. I haven't seen Larkin or O'Hearn since, and what're they thinking I said?"

Kintyre didn't look at Corinna, he didn't believe it would be decent for a minute or two. He asked Guido: "What other jobs did you do for these men? Rent a house for them?"

"No — nothing. I turned the car back to the rental agency on Monday, that's all. They'd advanced some of my expenses. They still owe me — "

"You're not likely to collect," said Yamamura. He nodded to Kintyre. "I see what you're driving at. They missed a bet, not having him rent the scene of the crime too. And of course it was a mistake to dump the body across the Bay: that expedited the investigation, rather than slowing it up as intended. But then, they were strangers to this locality. And there's not much long-range difference, is there?"

"What do you mean?" asked Guido lifelessly.

"I mean you've been played for an all-time sucker," said Kintyre. "It's pure luck — the Michaelises just happened to become Patsy Number One — that you haven't been arrested on suspicion of murder. So far."

He heard Corinna gasp. Guido seemed too drained to understand.

"Another thing," said Kintyre. "What's between you and Gerald Clayton?"

"Clayton?" The empty eyes blinked from the bed. "Clayton. Oh, him. Nothing."

"Are you certain?"

"We talked for a while, up at his pad. Bruce took me there. So finally he gave me the polite brush-off and I came on over here to do my show. Bruce stayed."

"That's all? You're sure?"

"For a long time, anyway. I met him once before — months and months ago — just social like — " Guido's tones dribbled to silence.

Kintyre rubbed his chin. "That seems to let Clayton off," he said. "If, to be sure, our friend here is telling the truth."

"He is," said Corinna. Turning, Kintyre saw her inhumanly composed. "I know him. He can't be lying now."

"I wish I could be that certain," said Kintyre. "The whole thing makes so little sense that — Though Judas, I feel I could almost grasp the answer, but no."

Yamamura asked Guido: "Where is this dope you brought?"

"It's not dope," said the figure on the cot: a tired, automatic protest. "It's only pod."

"Never mind that. If you don't like the law, write your Congressman. Where's the dope?"

"They'll kill me if — "

"What use is your life to you right now?" asked Yamamura scornfully.

It had not seemed possible Guido could shrink further into himself. "That dressing table over there," he whimpered.

Yamamura opened the drawer, flipped out a small parcel, and tore a corner. "Uh-huh," he said.

"Well?" said Kintyre.

"Well, by rights we should turn this and the kid in. It could mean a stretch in a Federal prison, since he crossed a border. It could even mean a loss of citizenship, he being naturalized. Dope is a hysterical issue."

Corinna did not speak.

Yamamura continued, in an almost idle tone: "However, it's true enough that this isn't a really vicious drug. I could heave it into the nearest garbage can and there'd be an end of the matter. If you think he's had a little sense beaten into him."

Kintyre said: "That's my guess, Trig." Yamamura slipped the package into a coat pocket. Corinna shuddered, her fingers closed about Kintyre's.

Yamamura knocked the dottle from his pipe, which had gone cold between his teeth, and said, "Let's assume for now that he is telling the truth. Then what have we got?"

"A couple of murderers still hanging around," said Kintyre. "Why? Surely not to collect their hashish. That was just a gimmick to make Guido, their decoy, leave town, and make it damn near impossible for him to explain why. Whether or not a murder charge could have been made to stick, it would certainly confuse the issue long enough for this job to be finished, for the killers to go safely home again, and for the one who hired them to cover his tracks completely."

"You imply their job is not yet finished," said Yamamura.

"I sure do. There's no other sane reason for them to stay around, risking detection and arrest. Only — who's next?"

"Guido?" It was Corinna who asked it, firmly.

"I doubt that, at least as far as the original plan went. Who wants a dead red herring? Of course, now they may indeed go for him, afraid of what he has spilled. I think we'd better take him across the bay."

Yamamura nodded. "Let's get moving," he said. "Up there, lad." He stepped to the cot, took Guido under the arms and hauled him erect. "We can go out the back door."

Guido shambled, leaning heavily on the detective. Kintyre and Corinna followed. "He must be telling the truth," she said. "I know him! And that package — "

"Does tend to bear out his yarn," said Kintyre. "I want to believe in his essential innocence myself. The trouble is, if his story is true, then who hired the killers?"

"That Mr. Clayton?"

"Not if Guido has given us a full and fair account. I've explained to you that the Michaelises are out. Who's left?"

"I've heard of a writer. Owens, is that his name?"

"I don't know. I plain don't. And yet I'm nagged by a feeling that I already have the answer —and I can't name it! Things have been happening too fast." Kintyre scowled. "And until we can identify the one who hired the killers — the real murderer; the others are only a deodand —he's free to murder someone else."

They had come down the stairs now, slowly, and stepped into the alley behind the building. Windowless brick walls closed three sides: it was a cul-de-sac thick with shadows, opening on a wanly lit trafficless street of hooded shops.

The man by the alley entrance stepped a little closer. There was just light enough to show that he was not tall, that he had sloping shoulders, and that he carried an automatic pistol. He stopped three yards from the door, too far off for a leap.

"Hold it," he said.

15

Yamamura and Guido had come out first. Guido's legs seemed to go fluid; only the arm around his waist held him up.

"Jimmy," he bleated.

Kintyre's hand swung backward in an arc, shoving Corinna behind him. He said aloud — very loudly, "What the devil do you want?"

"Quiet, there," said the man called Jimmy. "This thing has a silencer on it." He waved the gun. "I want to see Lombardi."

"It isn't nothing, Jimmy," chattered Guido. "Before God, Jimmy, they're just friends of mine!"

"Yeh. You can tell us all about it. The rest of you stand back against the door. Come on, Guido. I got a car waiting."

Yamamura eased his burden to the ground. Guido huddled on hands and knees, retching. "He'll never make it," said the detective. "He's scared spitless."

"I just want to talk with him," said Jimmy. "I was supposed to see him here tonight, only they said he'd gone upstairs. I figured if it was just for a nap or something, he'd be down again to finish his act and I'd catch him later. Only if he wanted to skip out this way instead, it would be soon and he might not come back. I didn't want to miss him, so I figured I'd wait here a while."

It was not meant as an explanation. It was an indictment, nailed word by word on the man who tried to stand up.

"Well," said Yamamura, "let me help him."

Jimmy laughed under his hat. "I'm not that simple-minded. Stay put." With shrillness: "Come on, Guido. Or do you want to get drilled right here and now?"

Guido began to drag himself forward, as if a bullet had already smashed his spine. The sound of it, and of his breath going in and out an open mouth, and the nearby clamor of automobiles filled with meek taxpayers, was all that Kintyre could hear.

He wondered if he could let Guido be taken from him, by the same instrument which had taken Bruce, and call himself male. Two or three jumps should reach Jimmy. But Jimmy was no amateur, he wouldn't miss if he shot. But there were many cases on record of men being hit once, twice, being filled with lead, and still coming on. But Guido wasn't worth anybody's time. But Guido was brother to Bruce and Corinna, therefore worth a great deal of time. But a possible forty years?

But a deeper shadow filled the open end of the brick gut. It ran forward in total silence, light touched its glassy uplifted club and its flowing hair.

As the bottle came down on Jimmy's head, Kintyre started to move. Yamamura beat him to it, arriving a second after Jimmy lurched forward from the impact on his skull. The sound had been a shattering; Kintyre heard the tinkles that followed the blow. Yamamura knocked the gun from Jimmy's hand with an edge-on palm, seized his lapel, and applied a scissor strangle.

Jimmy fell, as if the bones had been sucked from him. Corinna swayed over his form, still holding the broken beer bottle. Almost, she fell too. Kintyre caught her.

She held him closely, shuddering. It was not necessary, he thought beneath his own pulse. She fought herself, and grew worn down thereby. Her physical output had been negligible. Clearly she had slipped back through the door, unobserved (that was the chance she took, but chance had a way of favoring those who acted boldly). Picking up an empty bottle on the way, tucking it inconspicuously under an arm, she had gone out past the bar, out the main door (doubtless noticed, maybe wondered about, but not stopped and soon forgotten) and around the building. Then she took off her shoes and ran up behind Jimmy and hit him.

That was all. There was no reason to grow exhausted. But God damn all smug judokas, hadn't she earned the right?

"You clopped him a good one," said Yamamura, squatting to look. "It's as well he had a hat on. A cut scalp could get very messy. Congratulations."

"Did you say there was a cop in the bar?" asked Kintyre.

"Beyond doubt," said Yamamura. "Or we can phone, of course. Only I'm carrying a parcel of smoke, and the neighborhood will be searched quite thoroughly if our friend here mentions it." He sat on his heels, chin in hand, for what seemed like a long time. Jimmy moaned, but did not stir.

"Bob," asked Yamamura finally, "do you know anyone living on this side who's mixed up in the affair?"

"Just Guido, if we rule out the Michaelises."

"So the big chief — and his next victim — are probably in the Eastbay. If another murder is to be forestalled, I wonder if we ought to spend time here chatting with a lot of well intentioned policemen who will first have to be convinced the Michaelises are innocent and this wasn't a simple stick-up. Especially when the papers will tell the big chief exactly what's happened. Or, even if they can be made to keep quiet, Jimmy will fail to report in; the gang will try to check for him in the San Francisco pokey, first of all; so we could do some trail-covering of our own."

"You mean to take this character to Berkeley, then? Isn't that pretty irregular? You don't want to jeopardize your license."

"It's as irregular as a German verb, and the police are going to be annoyed. But I do think we can flange up enough excuses to get by with it. Of course, the Berkeley force will call up the San Francisco force immediately, but that'll go on a higher level, chief to chief I imagine; we can explain the need for secrecy, as much secrecy as the law allows, and — Hell, Bob, let's stop mincing words. What we need is time to construct a story that'll cover Guido. And you."

Kintyre felt how the stone-rigid body he held began to come alive again. "Blessings," he murmured.

"We'll go to your place first, and then decide what's next."

"Can you finagle Jimmy across the bridge?"

"Him and Guido both," grinned Yamamura. "Which will leave you a clear field when you take the lady home."

"I'm coming," said Corinna. She pulled herself away from Kintyre, gently.

"You are not," he answered. Seeing in the dirty gray half-light how her face grew mutinous, he went on: "There are enough complications already. What could you do over there, except be one more element we have to explain away — or one more target for the gang? At present, only Jimmy knows you have any concern with this business, and he'll get no chance to talk of it."

She thought on his words for a little. Then: "Yes. You're right. But don't drive me all the way. A taxi will — "

"Shut up!" he laughed, shakily, and took her arm.

They had to wait, guarding a half-conscious prisoner, while Yamamura went after his car. Guido sat on the pavement, knees drawn up under his chin. After a while he took out a cigarette and lit it.

Corinna leaned over him. "Go with them," she said. "They're the only real friends you've got."

"Besides you, sis," he muttered. Then, barking a sort of laugh: "Next week, East Lynne."

She sighed, like an old woman, and stood back again.

Yamamura returned and bound Jimmy's wrists with Jimmy's tie. He and Kintyre frogmarched their captive to the Volkswagen and put him in back on the floor. Yamamura secured his ankles with his belt. "Toss me your house key, Bob, I'll see you there. Hop in, Guido. Cheerio."

Kintyre and Corinna walked hand in hand back toward his own car. They stopped to pick up her shoes. "I'm afraid you ruined your stockings," he said inanely.

"You don't have to talk," she said. "I don't need it."

He was grateful for that. The silence in which they drove home (she did not lean against him, but she sat close by) was somehow like — memory groped — like Bruce's music which Margery had played for him a few centuries ago. He wondered if she had heard it yet.

"I hope you'll be able to sleep," he said at her door.

"Oh, yes, I think so." She considered him and asked gravely: "Why are you doing this for us?"

"I can't stop now," he said. "I'm in up to the eyebrows."

"But why did you begin? Not for Bruce's sake, surely. He wouldn't have cared about being avenged."

"Which is what the police are for, anyway. I don't like this evading them that we've been forced into."

"Well?" she continued.

"Why do you want to know?" he dodged.

Her head drooped. "I suppose it isn't any of my business. I'm sorry."

It hammered within him to tell her: that he had been escaping a demon, that she had worn its shape for a single moment, and that now he wanted to give peace to her. But there had been too many locks in him, for too many years.

He took her hand. "Later," he said, wondering if he meant it. "This is no time for a long, involved story."

"I'll stay home tomorrow," she said. "Will you call me as soon as — anything happens? The first minute you're able to?"

"Of course."

She smiled then, reached up and ran her palm along his cheek. "Arrivederci," she said. The door closed behind her.

It was so much more than he had awaited, that he never remembered going down the stairs. He was driving over the bridge before the complete bleakness of his purpose returned.

The hour was not yet midnight, but Berkeley was quiet. Kintyre parked behind Yamamura's Volks and walked around the empty house to his cottage. The detective let him in.

"Where are our friends?" asked Kintyre.

"Guido is in your bed, snoring," said Yamamura. "As clear a case of nervous exhaustion as I ever saw. By the way, Jimmy's name is O'Hearn; I went through his billfold. I borrowed some of that rope you've been making grommets with and stashed him in the john."

He had stripped off his jacket, to show a noisy aloha shirt; his pipe strove to be Vesuvius. "Are you very tired?" he asked.

"No. Keyed up, in fact."

"Have a drink. Apropos vices, the evidence against Guido is in the Bay. I assumed we're not going to hand him over to the law."

"Not for one bit of foolishness," said Kintyre. "I doubt if he'll ever touch dope running again. He's gotten a hefty scare."

"Jimmy will tattle, though."

"Our word against his. We're somewhat more respectable."

"You and Machiavelli! But, yeh. A check with the Chicago police — he's from there, all right — would doubtless show he's got a record as long as King Kong's arm. A pro killer doesn't come out of nowhere; he starts with petty stuff and works his way up." Yamamura shook his head. "And on the other hand, a lot of good men are doing time for one slip regretted the moment it was over. Makes me wonder about our whole concept of penology. That's why I'll help you cover for Guido."

Kintyre took down his bottle of Scotch and raised brows at Yamamura. The detective shook his head. Kintyre poured for himself and sat down. The other man prowled.

"We haven't much time," said Yamamura. "What do we tell the cops?"

"Perhaps nothing — yet," said Kintyre slowly.

"Huh? How do you mean?"

"They don't use the third degree around here. O'Hearn isn't going to tell them a thing, and you know it. They'll have to check with Chicago, the FBI, follow a dozen separate leads for days at least. And what do his pals do meanwhile?"

Yamamura stopped in midstride. "If you have any half-cooked scheme of beating the truth out of him, forget it," he said in a chill voice.

"Oh, no," said Kintyre. "But do you think we could get away with holding him, unharmed, for maybe twenty-four hours?"

"It would be kidnaping."

"What was he trying to do to Guido?"

Yamamura stared at the sabers on the wall. "What do you want to do?"

"Get his information out of him in less time than the police will need."

"I think an excuse could be manufactured," said Yamamura dreamily. "If not for a whole twenty-four hours, for twelve or so. This reminds me of my days in OSS. Okay, I'll risk it."

"Good," said Kintyre. "Then follow my lead."

"Better explain —"

Kintyre was already in the bathroom, looking down at the man on the floor. O'Hearn had a long nose and not much chin. "Who hired you, Jimmy?" said Kintyre.

Hatred glared back at him. "Tough, aren't you?" said O'Hearn. "Big deal."

"I asked who hired you," said Kintyre.

He saw the growth of fear. "Look, I don't know," said O'Hearn. "And if I spilled anything, anything at all, they'd find out."

"And kill you. I've heard that line before." Kintyre shrugged. "You are going to tell me. Think about it while I make ready."

He took Yamamura out into the yard, toward the house. "My landlord left some extra keys with me, just in case," he said. "We'll borrow a soundproof room."

"Hey!" Yamamura stopped. "I told you, bodily harm is out."

"I've no such intention." Kintyre led him into the house and down to its basement. "We'll use the rumpus room. It has a pool table we can tie him to. The process seems to work best when the victim lies supine. I admit he might get a little stiff from the hard surface."

Yamamura grabbed his shoulder. "What the blue hell are you talking about?" he growled.

"They're just now beginning to study the mental effects of eliminating sensory stimuli," said Kintyre. "The mind goes out of whack amazingly fast. My friend Levinson, in the physiology department, was telling me about some recent experiments. Volunteers, intelligent self-controlled people who knew what it's all about and knew they could quit any time they wanted — none of which applies to O'Hearn — didn't last long. Hallucinations set in. Of course, we may have to mop up certain messes afterward."

"Do I understand you rightly?"

"I suppose so. The only thing we're going to do to O'Hearn is tie him down, flat on his back, blindfolded."

They would have to stand watch and watch outside the door. Kintyre took the first one, though he didn't expect a reaction soon. (On the other hand, an hour can stretch most hideously when you are alone in soundless dark, not even able to move.) He pulled up a chair and opened a book, but didn't read it. Nor did he listen to the defiant obscenities which came very faintly through the panels. Mostly he sat in a wordless half sleep.

Corinna, he thought. And then, later: *I'm being infantile. It doesn't mean a thing, except that I've been celibate too long and by sheer chance she pushes a few buttons in me. It could not last — consider the difference in faith alone — and she would be hurt.*

How do I know it wouldn't, even to the altar? (For surely it would last always, having taken us that far.)

I don't know. I suppose I'm being cowardly in not finding out.

Then again, long afterward: *This couldn't be hurried in any event. We'd both go slowly, her loss is still so new. There'd be ample time for me to escape, before the pleasure of her presence became a necessity.*

And once more: *But why should I want to escape at all?*

The first thin gray was stealing over the hills when Yamamura yawned his way in. O'Hearn hadn't cried out for some time; he lay breathing hard. "Solved the case yet?" asked Yamamura. "No? Well, run along and let a professional handle it."

Kintyre went across the yard. A bird twittered somewhere, drowsily. He entered the cottage and looked at Guido. Still out. The face was gone innocent with sleep, years had been lost, a della Robbia angel lay in his bed. He sighed, kicked off his shoes, and stretched on the living room couch. Darkness was quickly upon him.

16

Once the phone rang. He rolled over, refusing its summons, and went to sleep again. It was a little after six when a hand shook him awake. He struggled up through many gray layers. From far off he heard: "Jimmy's broken. Busted into pieces all over the place. Hoo, what a devil you are, my friend!"

Kintyre sat up, feeling sticky. Yamamura gave him a lighted cigarette and he took a few puffs. "Okay," he said.

The early sunlight and the rushing sound of early traffic whetted him as he left the cottage, until he went clear-brained to the shivering, screaming thing on the pool table and said: "I'll take the blindfold off when you've talked. Not before."

"Let me go, let me go, let me see!" wept O'Hearn.

"Shut up or I'll leave you for another day or two," said Kintyre.

O'Hearn gasped himself toward a kind of silence.

"Did you help kill Bruce Lombardi?" asked Kintyre.

"No." A cracked whine. "I mean, I was there. But the others, Silenio, Larkin, they done it. I didn't touch him myself. Let me out of here!"

"Shut up, I told you." Kintyre drew deeply on his cigarette. "I suspect you're lying about your own role," he continued, "but never mind that now, if you don't lie on the next question. Who hired you?"

"I don't know!"

"So long," said Kintyre.

"I don't know! I don't! They never told me! Silenio knows! I don't! I just worked for Joe Silenio! Ask him!"

Yamamura, looking a little sick, said: "That's probably true, Bob. Our kingpin called this Silenio in Chicago, and Silenio rounded up a couple of assistants. The less they know, the better. Silenio gets the kingpin's money and pays off the other two himself."

Kintyre groaned. "And we had to catch one of the deadheads! Well, let's see what else can be learned."

It came out in harsh automatic sentences. O'Hearn's will, never strong, had altogether failed him. He answered questions without evasions, but like a robot.

Silenio had contacted him and Larkin the Tuesday of last week. It was to be a well paid job, ten thousand dollars on completion of the first assignment and a hundred dollars a day while they waited for the next. ("No, I didn't know nothing, I don't know who else we'd go after!") The trio caught a plane to San Francisco that night. At intervals on Wednesday and Thursday Silenio had conferred with whoever engaged them, while Larkin and O'Hearn looked for a suitable house. Their find was rented on Friday, an old house in a run-down district at the southern end of town; and each of them bought a good used car elsewhere. Meanwhile, on Thursday night, Larkin and O'Hearn had lined up Guido. That had been at Silenio's orders, presumably derived from the boss's. The boss himself had arranged for Bruce to come to the house on Saturday, calling him on the phone with some plausible story. They captured Bruce very simply, with a gun, and tied him up. Silenio questioned him. Bruce had gotten stubborn with outrage — Kintyre knew how stubborn that could be — and the interrogation took a few hours; even after he broke they continued the pain a while, to make sure. Finally they cut his throat over the bathtub, dressed him in old clothes, and got rid of the body across the Bay on Sunday night.

"The questions, you bastard," snarled Kintyre. "Didn't the questions Silenio was asking tell you something?"

"It was all in wop," groaned O'Hearn. "I don't know wop."

Italy again. Though I suppose that our X would have made a special effort to get an Italian-speaking lieutenant, as another safeguard for himself.

"One thing so far," murmured Yamamura. "Guido is in the clear."

"Is he?" said Kintyre bitterly. "Wouldn't it be a beautiful turnabout, to make himself look like the fall guy for his own scheme?"

He turned back to the crooked blind face on the table. "What did you do afterward?"

"Waited in the house. Played cards. Silenio got the money for this job in the afternoon. Cash. He went out for it. Larkin went to pay off the Lombardi sucker Tuesday evening. That was because he didn't show Monday, account of his brother. Larkin got into a fight. We didn't know what it meant. Silenio called the boss and they talked on the phone in wop. Silenio told me to go pick up Guido Lombardi tonight. I figured we was going to find out how much he knew and then maybe dump him too, but I don't know for sure."

"Did anything else go on, this night?"

"Silenio and Larkin had another job."

"Where?"

"I don't know." The voice had become a worn rattling.

"Were you supposed to meet them at the house?"

"I was supposed to wait there with Lombardi till they got back. Silenio wasn't telling either of us more'n he had to."

"Will they be back there now?"

"I dunno."

"Suppose they came back and didn't find you? What would they do?"

"Try and find out what happened, I guess. Wouldn't stay in the house if it looked like something had gone wrong."

"Where would they go?"

"I don't know. Some hotel, I guess."

"And what would you do, if you couldn't find them?"

"Go back to Chi, I guess."

"No spare rendezvous," said Yamamura. "Lousy doctrine."

"Not if you're using expendables," said Kintyre. "And this bum is expendable. I imagine Larkin is too, though enough more valuable to go with Silenio — where?"

"Over here," said Yamamura.

"Very likely to kill someone else." Kintyre looked dully at the stub of his cigarette on the floor. He didn't remember dropping it. "We'll read in the papers who it was."

"If we aren't the target ourselves," said Yamamura. "Right now anything seems possible." He sighed. "Well, I'd better call the police."

"Wait a bit," said Kintyre.

"But that house — God knows what's going on there, right now!"

"Nothing, I'm sure. If only because Silenio and Larkin will be worried by O'Hearn's absence. Let's have breakfast, at least, before calling. You devise a story that won't make us quite such lawbreakers. I'm going to try and sort out my thoughts. I have an idea. It's driving me crackers, Trig. I feel I know what this is all about and still there's some kind of wall between me and the knowledge. A wall I've built myself."

"Hm," said Yamamura. He gave the other man a meditative stare. "Yes, it might be worth while waiting till after we eat."

Kintyre went out, beating a fist softly into his palm. Yamamura paused to release O'Hearn's eyes. O'Hearn lay and wept.

While the detective made breakfast in the cottage, Kintyre took a shower. Then a shave, clean clothes, tee shirt, khaki pants, tennis shoes, brought him physically closer to humanness.

Inside, he was afraid, and he did not know why.

Guido appeared in the kitchen as Kintyre re-entered. He looked at the others with deer shyness. "Good morning," he ventured.

"Hello," said Yamamura. "Pull up an egg and sit down."

Guido perched on a chair's edge. No one spoke until coffee and food were within them. Somehow, the blue and green planet beyond the windows had become alien; they sat in a private darkness.

"I — " began Guido. He stopped.

"Go ahead," said Yamamura. Kintyre listened with a fractional ear. Mostly he was inside his own skull, shouting for something which did not answer.

"I'd like to say thanks, is all," offered Guido.

"It's okay," said Yamamura.

"Look, are you sitting and worrying about me?"

"In a way. The trouble is, you see, if we take your story at face value, we have no plausible suspects left. But two more killers and their chief are loose, probably arranging another murder. If it hasn't already been done."

"Whose?" whispered Guido.

"If we knew that," said Yamamura gloomily, "we could get a police guard for him. But until we've identified the chief, there's no way of figuring who the next victim might be."

"No," said Kintyre.

He sat up straight, feeling how cold his hands were. It came to him, through a great hollowness — each instant he seemed more remote from himself — that he could have found his enemy before now. He had enough facts to reason on. He was still feeling his way a step at a time, but he felt there would be an end to his journey.

And he felt, without yet knowing why, that the horror waited for him there.

He said, sensing a resonance within his head, as if his voice formed echoes:

"It has to be someone who knew Bruce at least fairly well. He went to that house because of a telephone call. He didn't own a car and wouldn't borrow Margery's. That's a long awkward trip, by street train and bus. He wouldn't make it casually. He'd want to know why he was being asked to come to this address he'd never heard of before, *without telling anyone*. The person who called (and could have been right in Berkeley, of course) had to be somebody who could give Bruce a strong, convincing reason. What it was, I don't know. It doesn't matter now, it was surely a lie. But a lie he would accept! From a person he trusted."

He stopped. Guido said with a certain boy-eagerness: "Who knew him best? His girl friend!"

Kintyre shook his head, violently, uncertain why the idea should smite him so.

"Nope," said Yamamura. "Too much lets her out; hell, the simple fact that she doesn't speak Italian. That she hasn't the money, or the connections, or anything."

"I haven't the money either," said Guido defensively.

"For all I know, you could have ten million dollars hoarded," said Yamamura.

The anger in Guido's face reminded Kintyre of Corinna. He snatched for the memory, it warmed him a minute and was torn away again. He shivered.

"Guido's story has to be accepted, I think," he said. There was no color in his words, but they came fast. "All the psychological quirks he's shown. He bopped me with a stool to let Larkin get away, because he was deathly afraid. But he cried at having hurt me, even so trivially. Also: could that parcel of marijuana have been in the drawer by sheer coincidence? And even if he planned some complicated misdirection that made him his own fall guy, it would not have involved something as serious as dope. He could have gone to jail for that, or been deported. And why? What reason? Insane jealousy won't fit such an elaborate procedure. It would have to be money. And where would he, drifting between minor night club engagements, sponging off his parents when he isn't shacked up with some tart, where would he find time for a million-dollar enterprise?"

Guido reddened. "Hey!" he protested.

"You had that coming," said Yamamura. He turned his back on Guido, who slumped, pouting. "It doesn't look as if X really believed an accessory-to-murder rap could be hung on the boy," he remarked. "Not when you demolish it so fast."

"Perhaps not." Kintyre struggled for clarity within himself. "But Guido would have wriggled and evaded much more if the police had questioned him, dug in his heels at every step, for fear of the dope charge. When he finally realized the situation and confessed, if he did at all, it would have been too late. He would have served X's purpose of holding up the police for days.

"And the fact that he fell so neatly into the slot clinches the proof that X knows the Lombardi family well."

"You've ruled out Michaelis & Son," said Yamamura. "That's confirmed by the gangsters still operating with them in clink. Who's left, the writer?"

Kintyre said: "He blew into town less than two weeks ago, having never met Bruce in his life before. Their time together was a few meetings devoted to professional arguments. How could he know Guido? And his only motive would have been to eliminate Bruce. Simple murder would have sufficed, not calling in three expensive sadists to do a job of kidnaping and inter-rogation. Also, I proved to myself, without meaning to, that he's a physical coward. I doubt if he could have asked someone like Larkin the time of day. Or run the risk of detection. No, there was just one way Owens helped the killers, and that was unintentional."

"How?" asked Yamamura.

Kintyre looked at his hands. They were clasped together, as if to hold the safe nonmurderer, Jabez Owens, tightly to him. But the wind streamed and the sea ramped beneath it, Owens was whirled from his fingers and drowned with all the rest, all the rest. He said from the noise of great waters:

"Owens was after the Book of Witches, yes. First he tried bribery. Then, the minute he heard Bruce was dead, he went over to the history building, I suppose trying to get up nerve to go in and see if the volume was there. He saw me instead, and urged me to take Margery out that night; he did know, like everyone else, that she'd been living with Bruce. He burgled the apartment. An amateur job. If he'd used his brains, he would at least have taken some valuables. But he didn't even bother to open places where the book couldn't possibly be. That alone pretty well shows who did it. He tried again yesterday, in my office, actually pulled it off, but Clayton — well, all it accomplished was to divert our attention."

He wondered remotely how they could fail to see what was happening to him; and how long before it broke his shell and they could not escape seeing.

"Bruce's immediate family?" said Yamamura. "No motive, no money, no connections, no opportunity. Write 'em off. Can you think of any of his friends at the University who aren't eliminated by the same reasoning?"

"No."

"But who's left? Clayton? What motive? And in all the months he's been here, I'd have an inkling if he weren't honest. No hint of underworld tie-ins. Who's left?"

Kintyre stood before the last wall. It had the form of a ship's tilted deck.

"If I knew why," he said, holding his voice utterly planar, "I think the how would follow. Why was Bruce killed? Because of something he knew. It could only be that. He was tortured to get out of him the precise extent of his knowledge, and who else might share it. That other person is the next victim. But what was in Bruce's background? A knowledge of history — the Book of Witches — correspondence with — " His throat seemed to swell, it would not let the words out for a moment — "with an uncle in Italy, who told him something — "

"Something about the Mafia?" snorted Yamamura. "Come, now!"

"Bruce didn't realize the significance of what he knew," said Kintyre. Iron bands lay across his chest. "He couldn't have kept a secret like that. He went to X, I suppose — with — a warning? Or mere gossip, as he thought? What about? Surely not Cousin Giovanni, or the Albigensians. What else was there? Some information on crime in the Mediterranean countries. And — God help us!"

The table went over with a crash as Kintyre stood up. It was not himself who screamed: "Margery! She's next in line!" Himself stood among breakers and heard the mainmast split.

Yamamura looked at him, cursed, and reached for the telephone.

"I'm going over there," rattled Kintyre. "I might get there first. I might, it might not be too late."

"They had all night," said Yamamura. His finger stabbed the dial.

Kintyre blundered into the door. He thought vaguely that he ought to open it. Someone stood at his elbow. He shoved. "Take it slow," said Guido. "Let me help you."

Yamamura said in the phone: "Tim? This is Trig. Never mind formalities. Get a car to the apartment of Margery Towne. She may still be alive....No, I don't remember the damned address! What's the directory for?"

"You're in no shape to steer a car," said Guido. "Where are your keys? Come on and guide me."

Kintyre sat shaking all the way over. Guido drove with a Cossack will to arrive at which a part of Kintyre, drowning among the reefs of Taputenea, knew dim surprise.

They did not beat the police, though. Officer Moffat met them on the front steps. Blankness lay in his gaze.

"We came too late," he said. "Her throat's cut."

"I expected that," said Kintyre.

The horror rose up and took him.

17

Jimmy O'Hearn was still snuffling when the police unbound him and led him off to be booked. Inspector Harries went back into the yard with Yamamura and Guido. "All right, Trig," he said, "now tell me just what did happen."

"Dr. Kintyre, Mr. Lombardi's sister, and I went to see Mr. Lombardi at the night club where he works," answered Yamamura. "He was pretty worried. O'Hearn and another chap named Larkin had hired him to do a certain out-of-town job over the very weekend his brother was killed. He wondered if it was a coincidence."

"O'Hearn babbled something about a package of dope," said Inspector Harries grimly. Guido became busy lighting a cigarette.

"Sure," said Yamamura. "Why not try to drag down the witnesses against him? Where is this package?"

"Suppose you tell me yourself what the job was, Mr. Lombardi," said Harries without warmth.

"Well, they did want me to go to Tijuana and get some pod," said Guido. Yamamura had briefed him in a moment's stolen privacy. "I admit I went down — is uncompleted intent a crime? I changed my mind and didn't actually get the stuff." Impudence danced over his lips. "It'd have been illegal. And also, thinking it over, I saw that the errand didn't make sense. There are enough places right here that carry the same line."

"Hm. Any witnesses?"

Guido shrugged. "No. How could there be? I suppose you can prove I was in Tijuana and ate a few meals there."

"I would think you'd have more important things to do than asking out the details of something which is contradicted only by the unsupported word of a gangster," said Yamamura.

Harries considered him angrily. "You were my friend, Trig," he said. "Don't add insult to injury."

"I had no choice," said Yamamura, very low.

"The night before last," said Guido, "Larkin showed up and got violent with Professor Kintyre, who was talking to me. Quite a brawl. Larkin got away, and Kintyre left too when I begged him. I admit I lied to the officers afterward, claiming I didn't know either one of them, but by then I was scared."

"Go on," grunted Harries.

"So we had a conference of friends-and-relations last night," said Yamamura. "We decided it was best to make a clean breast with the police. Ahem, that was my advice. But O'Hearn stopped us at gun point as we came out the back way. He was going to kidnap Mr. Lombardi. We got the upper hand, though. Yes, we took him over here, instead of turning him in to the San Francisco authorities as we should have. Why? First, Larkin might well be hanging around, and why should he be helped by seeing a lot of uniforms and realizing what had happened to his buddy? Second, we were afraid for our lives on that side and wanted to get the hell away from there."

Harries gave him a thin look. "I know you. I don't believe that."

"A jury would," said Yamamura. "Let me go on. Dr. Kintyre took Miss Lombardi home — she's entirely innocent in all of this. When he finally arrived here, we were so bushed that none of us thought we could face all the questions without a little sleep. Sure, sure, Inspector, everything we did was foolish and mildly illegal, but consider how exhausted we were. Much too tired to think straight. We tied O'Hearn to the table — "

"Why the blindfold, for Pete's sake?"

"It just seemed like a good idea. When we woke up, we found O'Hearn had the screaming meemies. Naturally we wouldn't lose such a chance, it might not come again. We asked him some things. We talked it over. All of a sudden the significance dawned on Dr. Kintyre. You know the rest."

"What I don't yet know is what you'll be charged with," said Harries. "Among other things, some of the coldest-blooded lying I've heard all week."

"Isn't that a problem for the district attorney?" asked Yamamura, unruffled.

"Yes. And of course nothing will be done. You're comic book heroes — for violating the Fifth Amendment!" Harries shook his head. "If it hadn't been for all your shilly-shallying, Miss Towne might be alive this morning."

"When was she killed?" asked Yamamura.

"The doctor thinks around midnight or one o'clock."

"Nobody could have known," said Yamamura. "Suppose we had turned O'Hearn in directly. He had no idea who was slated to die: not even what kind of job his associates were doing. He's just a goon."

"I suppose so." As he watched, Yamamura saw the anger go out of Harries. "We'd still be interrogating him and getting no place. Whereas now, maybe the San Francisco force can take the others in that house." The inspector hesitated. "Officially, I can only condemn your actions, including your concealment of facts. And you know I know fairly well what those facts are. I'll have to report all this and — and hell, there's no material evidence, and the D.A. has to consider public opinion, and why waste funds on petty charges which would never get past a jury? You'll get away with it this time. And strictly unofficially, I've no right to say it, but I guess I'm not too damn mad at you."

Yamamura did not smile. "I wish Bob could see it that way," he answered.

"What's the matter with him, anyhow?"

"A bad nervous spell. He gets them once in a while."

"Just like that?" asked Guido.

"No," said Yamamura. "It looks like a sudden collapse, but it isn't. He worked hard through the academic year. It brought him close to the edge, he needed a vacation badly. Instead, all this strain and — He feels morbidly responsible. There are reasons for it. They lie in his past and don't concern us."

"How about a psychiatrist?" inquired Harries.

"He hasn't got that kind of money. And we all have some such curse — don't we now? Some people have dizzy spells. Some people are hypochondriacs. Once every couple of years, Kintyre spends a few days in hell."

"But what made him realize Miss Towne was — ?"

"He answered the riddle, of course. He knew who had hired the killers, and why. From that, it followed she was next."

Harries caught his arm so tightly he winced. "What?"

"Uh-huh," said Yamamura. "Wait, though. He didn't tell me."

"But he's in there now and — come on!"

Yamamura caught Harries by the shoulder and spun him around. "No," he said. "It isn't right. Leave him alone."

"Leave the murderers alone, too!" snapped Harries.

Yamamura rubbed his chin. They could see how he slumped.

"There is that," he agreed. "Let me go in by myself, then, and talk to him."

Kintyre thought he had carried it off very well. He had spoken coherently with Moffat. The policeman told him in a sick voice that blood had soaked through her mattress until the floor was clotted beneath her bed. Guido swayed on his feet. Kintyre's face had remained like carved bone.

"Was jewelry lifted this time?" he asked. "Oh, yes, it was a professional job, all the earmarks," said Moffat. "But did you see two long gray cardboard boxes with files of papers? They'd be in plain sight in the living room if they're there at all," said Kintyre. "No, no such thing, the burglars must have taken them in the hope of finding stowed cash," said Moffat. "The jewelry was only to make you think that. Had she simply been murdered, or was she tied down first?" asked Kintyre. "Yes, tied down, blindfolded, mouth full of towel," said Moffat. "The burglars came in and grabbed her while she slept, secured her so there would be no chance she could identify them," said Kintyre. "That's not unheard of, but then why did they kill her afterward?" asked Moffat. "Because the letter boxes were still open on the coffee table," said Kintyre. "What?" said Moffat. "It proved she had been reading Bruce Lombardi's mail; the burglars' orders were to get rid of her if that was the case," said Kintyre. "Hey, how do you know all this?" asked Moffat. But then Kintyre felt his control begin to crack, so he turned about and went back to his car with Guido.

He lay on his couch, pillowing his head with an arm, a cigarette in the free hand. Now and then he noticed himself smoking it. The morning streamed in through the window behind him and splashed light, and the delicate shadows of leaves, on the wall before his eyes. Once he remembered how a sunbeam, spearing through a sky roiled and black with oncoming rain, had flamed from crest to crest along the ocean; he watched the sun's shining feet stride past him. But there followed an M which staggered among hideous winds, it spoke of Morna and Margery and the Moon. He spent a long time wondering why M stood for the Moon until he remembered Hecate, in whose jaws he lived. M was also for Machiavelli, a Moldering skull which knew somewhat of Murder. But all this was not important, it was Morbid and he only played with it on the surface, as if it were spindrift driven by that wind he knew. In the ocean of his damnation there were green Miles, which became black as you went downward, drank all sunlight and ate drowned folk.

This, however, was natural and right, life unto life and he could wish no better ending for himself than to breathe the sea. It must be remembered, though, that Morna was only thirteen years old. She reached for him through a shattering burst of water. He could not hear if she screamed, the wind made such a haro, but a wave picked her up and threw her backward and growled. He saw her long hair flutter in its white, blowing mane. Then dark violence rolled over him.

He stirred, and felt that his cigarette had gone so short it would burn his fingers. A part of him suggested he let it, but he ground the butt out in an ashtray on the floor. What he was would not be lessened by a few blisters, he thought.

It was not that he accepted guilt (he told the morning gulls on the reef, among sharded timbers). It was that he was damned, without a God or a Devil to judge him: it was merely in the nature of things that he did nothing well. Morna should drown and Margery should drown — the human body held that much blood — because — *no*, said the seed of survival within him, not because it was his fault.

And was there anything more irrelevant than the question of his guilt or innocence? The sole fact that mattered was:

Morna, thirteen years old, hauled down under the sea and rolled across a barnacled reef. He had found her washed up the next morning, before the boat came out to rescue him. A strand of hair still clung in place, darkened by water but more bright than the coral. He saw some of the bones; a tiny crab ran out of her eye socket.

Kintyre hung onto the couch through a whiteness that hummed.

Ages afterward he remembered Margery. She had never spoken of it, but he had an impression that she feared death. It ended future and past alike, nothing would be, nothing had ever been. She must have told herself often enough that maybe science would find a way to make her immortal, before she died. But death was a long way off, fifty years or more were a distance which dwindled the shape, only a small black blot on the edge of her world.

She lay blind and bound, a towel choking her mouth. She could hear her heart, how it leaped, she feared it would crack itself open. And then the hand under her jaw, the nearly painless bite of the knife, and the minutes it took for her blood to run out, while she lay there and felt it!

"No," said Kintyre. "No, no, no. Please."

He reached hazily for another cigarette. He couldn't find the pack. Suddenly he was afraid to look for it. He lay back on the couch. The sunlight on the wall seemed unreal.

He didn't hear Yamamura come in. He needed a while to understand that the detective was looking at him.

"What is it?" he got out somehow.

"Let's work some of that stiffness out," said Yamamura.

Kintyre didn't move. He wasn't sure he could. At least it didn't seem worth while. Yamamura swore, hauled him to a sitting position, peeled off his tee shirt and dumped him on the rug.

The Japanese massage, thumbs, elbows, and bare feet, was hard, cracking muscles loose from their tension. Kintyre heard joints pop when Yamamura straightened his arms. Once anguish got an oath from him.

"Sorry," said Yamamura. "I gauged wrong."

"Like hell! You did that on purpose!"

"Trade secrets. Now, over on your side."

In half an hour Kintyre was sitting on the couch, drawing ragged gulps of smoke down his lungs. "All right," he said. "So you relaxed me physically."

"Helps, doesn't it?" Yamamura leaned against the wall and mopped his sweating face.

"Some. But no cure." Kintyre looked bleakly toward the afternoon and the night.

"Didn't claim it was. Got any tranquilizers on hand?"

"Uh-huh. Only helps a little bit. I might as well ride these things out."

"Same symptoms?"

"Yes. Futility. Loss. Destruction. Grief? No, that's too healthy a word. I'm only talking to you with the top of my brain now, you realize. It feels the same as ever, down below."

"Basically, you feel guilt," said Yamamura.

"Perhaps. I saw my sister drown. I was hanging onto a spar when the ship broke up. She was swept past me. I reached out, our fingers touched, then she was gone again. I didn't let go of the spar."

"If you had, both of you would have drowned. I know the Pacific surf. With a typhoon behind it — You're guilty of nothing except better luck than she had."

"Sure," said Kintyre. "I've told myself the same thing for twenty years."

"You've told me this story three times so far," said Yamamura. "I don't like parlor Freudianism, but it would seem obvious that something deeper is involved than the mere fact that you survived and she didn't."

Kintyre half rose. He felt the lift of rage within himself. "Be careful!" he shouted.

Yamamura's face went totally blank. "Ah-ha. Sit back, son. I'm still the black belt man here. You'd only succeed in tearing up this nice room."

Kintyre spat: "There was nothing!"

"I never said that. Of course there was nothing improper. I am not implying you had any conscious thoughts whatsoever that you can't safely remember. Or if you did now and then — and as for your subconscious wishes — were they really so evil? She was the only girl of your generation whom you'd see for weeks and months at a time. So you loved her. Is love ever a sin?"

Kintyre slumped. Yamamura laid a hand on his shoulder. "There's a story about two Zen Buddhist monks who were walking somewhere," he said. "They came to a river. A woman stood by the bank, afraid to cross. One of them carried her over. Then the two monks continued on their way. The gallant one was singing cheerfully, the other got gloomier and gloomier. Finally the second one exclaimed: 'How could you, a monk, take up a woman in your arms?' The first one answered: 'Oh, are you still carrying her? I set her down back at the ford.'"

Kintyre didn't move. "Forgive my amateur psychoanalysis," said Yamamura. "It's none of my business." He paused. "I would only suggest that it's no service to anyone we've cared for, not to let them rest."

He sat down beside Kintyre and took out his pipe. They smoked together for a wordless while.

"Well," said Kintyre at last. "Have you figured out who's behind the murders?"

"No. Think you can tell us? Feel free to wait."

"Oh, I can. M-m-m-m-*margery* — "

Yamamura worked powerful fingers along Kintyre's shoulders and the base of his neck. "Go on," he said.

"Margery's death — brought back Morna's, I suppose — I failed them both. I didn't need O'Hearn's story to determine who instigated all this. I could have told you yesterday afternoon, if I'd used my head — *Ouch!*"

"That," said Yamamura, "was to halt an incipient tailspin. I felt it coming. You are not to blame for one damn item except being human and therefore limited, fallible, and unable to do everything simultaneously on roller skates. If you forget that again, I shall punch you in a more sensitive spot. Now why don't you go swallow one of those chemical consolations?"

"I told you they don't help much."

"I've no high opinion of 'em myself, but do so anyway."

When Kintyre had returned and sat down again, Yamamura said: "Okay, carry on. Who is our man?"

18

"Clayton," said Kintyre.

"Huh?" The pipe almost dropped from Yamamura's hand. "What the hell! Why, for God's sake?"

"Bruce got too much information about Clayton's rackets."

"What rackets? Clayton's straight! I never heard a hint — "

"Oh, yes. He's straight enough on this side of the Atlantic."

Yamamura muttered something profane. "How do you know?" he added.

'It fits the facts. Bruce was corresponding with his uncle Luigi, the secret service man. Some discussion of highly organized postwar crime syndicates in the Mediterranean countries came up. Now Clayton was a go-getter type who'd lost everything he had three times in a row: the Depression, his first wife's death, divorce from his second wife. It must have embittered him, so that he determined he would never again be poor and defenseless. He came to Italy as a Quartermaster officer in the war. Perfect chance for black marketing, if a man didn't mind taking a few risks. The miracle is not that a few QM people went bad but that most stayed honest. Clayton probably started in a very small way with cigarettes and K rations. But by the end of the war he was in touch with some pretty big figures in the Italian underworld, and saw the opportunities. He came right back after his discharge and went to work at it full time.

"Obviously, he's a hell of a good organizer. He got in on the postwar reconstruction of crime, along lines borrowed from gangland and Communism. He probably set out as a currency black marketeer, working through Switzerland. He soon expanded into other things, smuggling, dope, prostitution, gambling, the works. He became rich."

"Have you any proof of all this?" interrupted Yamamura.

"Chiefly, that it and only it will fit the facts. Let me go on, I'll fill in evidence as I proceed. The trouble with Clayton's riches was, they were mostly in lire, French francs, and other soft valuta. Also, governments all get nosy about resident aliens; he couldn't hope to avoid suspicion forever, without a good cover. He solved both his problems by becoming an importer. He bought European goods with his European money, shipped them over here, and sold them for dollars. On this side he's lily white, and familiar with prominent Americans of unquestionable integrity. Knowing this, Europeans don't think he might be something else on their continent. You can imagine the details."

"Yes," said Yamamura. "I can."

'Now for some facts as well as theories. Let's go back to Uncle Luigi. He's trying to break these syndicates, one of which is headed by the eminent Signor Clayton. Of course, because of its cell organization, Luigi and his colleagues don't know that. If they did, they could crack a lot of rackets open. All they have against Clayton is that a few of his business associates have bad associates of their own, notably some of the deported Italian-American gangsters. But what of it? Everybody outside a monastery must know some dubious characters.

'Well, because Clayton came here to work at opening a San Francisco branch, and because he brought the *Liber Veneficarum* along, he got to know Bruce. In fact, they came to be on very friendly terms. Clayton is genial enough, if you don't get in his way. Uncle Luigi, being somewhat anti-American, insisted that Signor Clayton had an unfair advantage, having started as a wealthy man with lots of dollars. That didn't fit with Clayton's own rags-to-riches story. Bruce got indignant, checked up, and established that Clayton had indeed been almost penniless when he came to Italy. And Luigi, as I mentioned before, had also happened to give Bruce some facts regarding crime, corruption, and the syndicates.

'I don't know just when Clayton learned about all this discussion. Perhaps a week ago last Sunday, when he saw Bruce over in the City and refused to give Guido a job. Clayton admits Bruce got mad; perhaps he said things then. Clayton smoothed his feathers and agreed to interview Guido next day. Maybe Clayton was already spinning a plan.

90

"Or it may have been amicable. Bruce had no reason to suspect Clayton of anything. We'd have known it otherwise; Bruce was constitutionally incapable of keeping a secret. Maybe in the love feast following his explosion, he blurted out how he had triumphantly refuted Uncle Luigi's sneers at the Horatio Alger rise of Gerald Clayton, and planned to send Uncle Luigi all the facts and demand an apology. At the same time, Bruce could have spoken about the syndicates. He was just naïve enough to have warned Clayton, who spent half his time overseas, to look out for the mobs! Well, one way or another, Clayton drew him out, doubtless in that conference they had after Guido was dismissed. Clayton was alerted."

It was peculiar, thought Kintyre, that he could talk so coolly while the horror was on him. But he had the horror locked away for this short time, he heard it speaking but did not really feel it.

"He could have pumped both brothers on Monday," nodded Yamamura. "Bruce in particular, but he would have seen how Guido might be made into a decoy — uh-huh. So he called a Chicago mob. But — "

"But why? Isn't it obvious, Trig? Bruce and Luigi were corresponding on two subjects which would explode if they were ever fitted together: Clayton and the Old World rackets. When Bruce revealed that Clayton had not, after all, started by depositing American dollars in Swiss banks, Luigi would begin to wonder. Bruce had even casually agreed that Clayton might have picked up a little loose change originally on the black bourse, which did not strike him as very heinous. Luigi might see deeper possibilities along those lines. Or things Luigi wrote could even make Bruce wonder, who knows? It wouldn't necessarily happen either way, but it was too big a risk to take. The American government itself, if it gets interested, has ways to check on its citizens abroad. So Bruce had to be eliminated. And he had to be questioned first, in detail, to learn precisely what he did know and who *else* knew. For instance, was Luigi already so well informed as to be dangerous? This was a job for professionals."

"And there's where your theory creaks," said Yamamura. "If Clayton is so law-abiding on American soil, where could he dig up his butcher boys on such short notice?"

"That hint was in Bruce's files," said Kintyre. "Your information about Clayton's telephoning adds detail. He must have called one of his not-very-respectable Italian associates. I seem to remember the name Dolce, you can try that on the switchboard girl for recognitionor. Does the phone office keep records of such things? I don't know. Let's assume he called Dolce, to give the man a name. He ordered him: 'Get hold of a recent deportee from America' — you can guess who better than I, Trig — 'and ask him how I can get in touch with a professional killer in this country.' He may have phrased it more euphemistically, but that was the sense of it. Next day Dolce or whoever called back. (Why else should a busy man like Clayton hang around home? Why not take the call in his office? Because his office deals directly with Italy, the switchboard girl there probably speaks the language and might eavesdrop.) Thus Clayton got the number of Silenio, and any passwords or the like that were needed. He went out to a pay booth and called him. O'Hearn has told us the rest."

Yamamura nodded. "Could be," he said.

"Tell me what else will explain the facts. And let me continue. Clayton came over here last Thursday on business, and threw a party in his suite for historians and literary scholars, including Bruce and me. I rather imagine he was looking for another red herring. Owens must have been promising. Not that Owens seems to have been jockeyed into anything, as Guido was, but Clayton dropped hints detrimental to him later on.

"Clayton made sure of being alibied the whole weekend. Of course, it was simple enough to make the call which lured Bruce to his death. He could have phoned from a pay booth right in sight of the world. I don't know what he told Bruce, probably that he might have something for Guido after all but it was confidential. Make your own lie.

"Monday he returned to the City. Silenio reported to him, got paid off, and was told to wait. Clayton had a problem: Bruce's files were still in Margery's apartment. Silenio would have learned that. Clayton had to choke off this last source of information. He came back here Tuesday and invited me to lunch with him. I gave him some idea of how well his tracks really were covered — and when I told him Margery's place had already been raided, it was a shock. He questioned me, found that the papers he was after were still unread, and deftly turned suspicion back on Owens: where for once it actually belonged. However, he must have felt the need to act fast. So he stayed in Berkeley, though he'd told me at lunch he planned to go back to San Francisco. (Will any hypothesis of yours explain why he changed his mind and spent more than twenty-four unproductive hours on this side? He, the animated cash register?) I met him again on Wednesday, when we had our run-in with Owens."

Kintyre sighed. "That's the damnable part of it. I sat there drinking coffee with the true, ultimate murderer. He urged me to take Margery out. I told him I had another engagement. If I had gone out with her, she'd be alive. God, if she'd dated him she might be! He was going to ask her. She told me, when I mentioned it, that she would refuse his invitation. He wanted to get her out of the way. But when she stayed —

"I helped her read those letters!"

"Slow down there," said Yamamura.

It was still later when the detective went back outdoors. An officer was watching Guido, who was laying out a solitaire hand on the stoop. The policeman said: "Inspector Harries would like to get a formal statement from you at headquarters, sir."

Yamamura nodded. Guido raised his brows and slanted his head at the cottage. "Could be worse," said Yamamura. "Suppose you leave him alone for an hour or so and then go in and make him some lunch."

"Sure," said Guido.

The policeman followed Yamamura out the drive. At the station, he was shown directly into Harries' office. The inspector was just laying down the phone. "San Francisco," he said. "They raided that address. Traces of occupancy, but nobody home."

"Any other news?" Yamamura sat down and folded his long legs.

"They let the Michaelises go. Gene broke down when they did — reaction, I guess — and admitted where he'd been Saturday night and Sunday. Shacked up."

"I wouldn't think he'd try to hide that. He'd have bragged."

"This time he had two metal legs and he paid. Not much, he hasn't got much, but he paid, for the first time in his life."

"Poor bastard. I can imagine how he feels."

"Well," said Harries, "what does Kintyre think?"

Yamamura told him.

Harries whistled. "That wouldn't even get past a grand jury," he said.

"It's a line worth further investigation, though," said Yamamura mildly. "I wonder where Clayton is right now?"

Harries snatched up the phone. Yamamura waited.

The inspector hung up with a bang. "Not at the Fairhill. I'll try his place in the City, and the office. Know the numbers?"

Presently: "Not there, either. Well, it's no crime. But I'll put a man on it."

"About releasing information to the press," said Yamamura. "Could you withhold any mention of Kintyre? He's in no shape to see reporters, or even tell them to go away."

"Glad to," said Harries. "We're going to sit on the facts as much as possible. We'll get the papers to cooperate. Why let the killers know what we know? They can guess we hold O'Hearn, but not that O'Hearn squealed."

"Good. Now let me make that statement so I can get back to my own office. Maybe a client has shown up, for a change."

None had. Yamamura polished his new sword. A thought nagged the back of his being. If Clayton was guilty, why should Clayton disappear? Harries was right, Kintyre's reasoning was skeletal. Without further evidence, it wouldn't be enough to arrest a dog for flea scratching. Clayton would do best to sit tight and be wronged righteousness.

But did he know that? O'Hearn had been sent after Guido merely because Larkin had gotten in a fight at the Alley Cat. If Larkin had not remembered the name "Kintyre" and reported it through Silenio, Clayton could still have made a shrewd guess at it. Yamamura picked up his own phone and dialed.

"Hi, Bob. How goes it?"

"I'm breathing," said Kintyre listlessly.

"Nobody at the murder house. Clayton has dropped from sight, too. You and Guido could be the next targets. Want a police guard?"

"No. He wouldn't be stupid enough to try for us just now," said Kintyre, without great interest. "Especially when he doesn't know how much I know. He would establish that first — yes, that would need his personal attention. Let's reconstruct it."

He voiced his thoughts as they ran, in flat metallic words. "Larkin and Silenio got back from their — their mission — and didn't find O'Hearn at the house. They waited till they got alarmed, then bolted and called Clayton in Berkeley. That would have been in the small hours, before sunrise. Clayton could have called the old Lombardis, pretending to be an anxious friend, and found Guido had not come home. The same pretense might have worked with the San Francisco police — nope, they had no word of any Guido Lombardi — no O'Hearn. He would also have drawn a blank in Berkeley. So. Somebody picked them both up. In view of the Alley Cat episode, he would suspect me. I remember now my phone rang, early in the morning. I didn't answer. Was that him, trying to check if I was at home? If he drove by, he'd have seen my shades pulled. He had no way of knowing O'Hearn was right here. He would have concluded: either I had nothing to do with it, or I had taken O'Hearn somewhere for private investigation.

"If he rubbed me out and I was innocent of meddling, well, too bad. He dared not assume anything except that Guido and I had O'Hearn — where? If he could track us down and dispose of us — of anyone who might finger him — yes, then later on he could bribe someone, a call girl perhaps, to give him a perjured alibi for the time involved, if any alibi was ever needed. Then nothing could ever be proved about his misdeeds on this side of the water. Of course, the Italian police and American foreign agents might be clued to his overseas work — but at worst he could stay home, or retire to some South American country that won't extradite him. But all this, avoiding arrest long enough to regain his balance, it all hinges on finding me —"

Kintyre's voice trailed off. Yamamura heard the receiver crash down.

Somewhat later his phone rang again. Kintyre said like a machine: "Trig, you can get the official ear quicker than I. Last night Corinna said she'd wait home till I called. I just did. There's no answer."

19

The Phone buzzed. Kintyre snatched it up. "Well?" he cried.

"Trig. Headquarters has just gotten word from San Francisco. Miss Lombardi isn't home. They checked inside with the superintendent's passkey. No trace of a ruckus. Couldn't she simply have gone out?"

"Look," said Kintyre. His vocal chords felt stiff. "This concerned her own family, herself — and O'Hearn, whom she had been forced to slug. I'd promised to call with the latest news. Would you have stepped out, even for a minute?"

"No. Of course, they queried her neighbors, parents, employer, and so forth. At last reports they were still getting nulls."

"Another thing," said Kintyre. "Clayton knew she saw me last night. I mentioned it to him yesterday afternoon!"

It whistled in his receiver. Then: "So you think he picked her up in the hope of finding out exactly where you are and what you know. Isn't that taking quite a risk?"

"For him, it's a greater risk to remain passive," said Kintyre. "Didn't we agree that if necessary he can probably buy a witness to account for a day or so absence? Though if Bruce, Guido, C-c-corinna, and I — Margery — if we've simply been found murdered, he might not even need that. There'll be no evidence to convict him."

"But why should he gamble his own precious hide? Let Silenio and Larkin do this job too."

"No. For one thing, Corinna might have been under protection already — God, if we'd had the brains to request it!"

"Mm, yes, I see. A gangster could ring her doorbell and pull a gun when she opened, and be nabbed the next minute if the police did have a stakeout. Clayton is a friend of her family; she'd invite him in and he could extract the gun in privacy after conversation had established it was safe to do so."

"That's it. Clayton doesn't know what we know. All he's sure of is that somebody has O'Hearn. He's got to find out who."

"Does it matter so much? O'Hearn doesn't know Clayton."

"But he knows Silenio, who does. Now suppose the police do have O'Hearn. They won't get the facts from him in a hurry, so there'll be time to dispose of those of us who Corinna tells Clayton know more than he likes. However, eventually the police will learn a few things, and in Chicago they'll be prepared to arrest Silenio and Larkin for questioning. So he'll have to give Silenio and Larkin a prolonged vacation somewhere, till the whole affair has blown over.

"On the other hand, if I am keeping O'Hearn, I can be expected to get rough. Therefore Clayton and his friends will have to act in an awful hurry. But if they succeed, all will be well for them: because I and any associates of mine will have been eliminated, in the course of rescuing O'Hearn, and no clues at all will be left for the police."

"Games theory," murmured the telephone. "You plan your strategy on the basis of the strategy your opponent would plan on the basis of the information you believe him to have. But this game is for keeps. What do you think we ought to do?"

"Throw out a dragnet, of course," said Kintyre. "As for the news angle, the knowledge we admit having — "

"That's an obvious one. The police can handle it. Though frankly, events will probably move so fast that our news releases won't influence them one way or another. Sorry, Bob, it had to be said.

"One more item. Now that their house is unsafe, have you any idea where they'll go?"

Kintyre groaned. "That's the one thing I can't even guess."

"You've done pretty well so far," said the gentle tone. "Need any help?"

"Yes," said Kintyre. "Get out there and find her."

"I'll do what I can," said Trygve Yamamura.

Kintyre hung up. Guido sat knotted about a kitchen chair. "Well?" he asked raggedly.

"You were listening," said Kintyre. "They've got her. Give me a cigarette."

"My sister," mumbled Guido.

Kintyre barked an obscenity. "Hell of a brother she's got," he said.

He lit up and stalked the kitchen floor. The clock said after eleven. Corinna had been taken — when? Three-plus hours ago, at a guess. But they would have had to find a place to question her. That would give a little time. They could conceivably be en route this minute.

"We're being a pair of prize schtunks," said Guido.

"Hm?" Kintyre threw him a look.

"Sitting here calling each other hard names. I mean, we ought to be out searching for her."

"Where?"

"Any place!" Guido's face was drawn taut; there was a tic over his right eye. "Every address we eliminate is something."

"How many houses in the Bay Area?" Kintyre flopped onto a chair. Through the doors he had locked in himself, the horror hooted.

"Well, for Chrissake, man," said Guido, "I don't mean to search the bishop's! We can think of some possible places, can't we?"

"I don't know."

"Ah, spit. We're doing nobody any good. Let's go for a ride. It might clear our brains some."

"The great American solution. Let's go for a ride."

Guido regarded Kintyre for a moment or so.

"Does it help you to feel superior, cat?" he asked quietly.

Kintyre's head jerked up. After a few seconds:

"Okay. I'll just phone in to let the police know we're going."

They left the cottage and Guido took the wheel of Kintyre's old black sedan. "Any special route, Doc?" he inquired.

"Oh, I don't know. The coast highway, southbound."

"State One? It's a bastardly slow drive beyond the freeway."

"What have we to hurry for?"

Guido slid the car into smooth motion. One-handed, he lit a fresh cigarette. "My solitary trick," he said wryly.

"You sing pretty well," said Kintyre.

"Not as well as I might. That takes work, and I'm not that interested."

"What are you interested in?" Kintyre responded mechanically.

"Right now, getting her back unhurt," said Guido. "Think there's a chance?"

"I thought we were going to clear our brains," rapped Kintyre.

They remained silent past the tollgate. Once they were on the bridge, with the quicksilver sheet of the Bay under them and San Francisco thinly misted ahead, Guido nagged:

"Where could they go? It'd have to be some place nobody would hear them, no cops would come around to. Pretty short notice to rent a house again. I mean, especially when an alarm might go out with their descriptions. Of course, they could just bust into a house offered to let."

"The police will be checking that."

"Uh-huh. Only Doc, wouldn't they expect it and try to outsmart the police? Dig me? Let's turn off at the ramp. I'm a waterfront kid, I know some old places where you could get in and — "

"Would they know about it?" snorted Kintyre.

"I suppose not." Crestfallen, Guido held the car in the middle lane. When they got onto the southbound freeway, he opened up.

Kintyre, a conservative driver, had never pressed his car to the limit. Now he saw the needle hover at ninety; wind snapped by the doors. "You want a ticket?" he asked.

"I don't much care," said Guido roughly. "Man, I got to do something, don't I? If I can't help her, I got to do something."

The minutes passed. No patrol car sirened at them. There was not, indeed, much traffic at this time of a Thursday. As they fled south, onto the old two-lane highway, the sky grew overcast.

"Nuts," said Guido. "There'll be fog along the coast. We'll have to crawl. Let's turn back."

"No," said Kintyre. "Keep going."

Guido stole an indignant look at him. "Wait a second," he began.

"Keep going, I said!" Kintyre roared it.

Guido started. Then, shrugging, he gave his attention back to the road. "Is it that important?" he asked.

Kintyre didn't answer because he didn't know. He sat hunched into passivity, not caring how fast they went or if they crashed. It shouldn't matter to him where he was taken. But it did. He couldn't tell why — *damn that fouled subconscious of mine, anyway!* But it was like a hand upon him.

Perhaps it was only that he had to get back for a while to the great shouting decency of the ocean.

"You're a funny one, Doc," said Guido after a long time.

"Aren't we all?"

"You're crazy, even for a human being. I mean, you're the cat who's had the adventurous life, got the culture, made the big success — oh, yes, you don't get paid much, but you know damn well how far you've succeeded and how much further you can go — you're everything Bruce wanted to be. Hell, you're everything I wish I wanted to be. And you can't wait to die!"

Kintyre said, jarred: "That isn't true. I'm just in a bad mood."

"So am I, Doc, so am I. Think I dare let myself imagine about Corinna? Think I enjoy realizing how poorly I've shown up in the last few days? But I keep going. What is it makes you fold up?"

Kintyre turned his face from the bluffs now humping up around him, toward Guido. There was a radiation of vitality from the other man; something had disfigured it, so that his days ran out in pettiness, but he would always be more alive than most.

"Why do you stay around here?" asked Kintyre slowly.

"Man, I like it."

"Can't you see it's poison for you? As long as you stay where you were a child, you'll always be one. If you could get away, you'd have a chance to grow up."

Guido reddened. "Thanks, Mother Superior."

"I'm not trying to insult you. I'm only thinking, your trouble could be caused by a situation. A place. Did you get overseas in the Army?"

"No, unless you count Alaska."

"And of course it wasn't your kind of life. All you'd think about would be going home. But suppose you went somewhere else, someplace congenial — and stayed. I wonder if you mightn't feel like buckling down. You could still make a name for yourself, or at least a fair living, as an entertainer. If you'd try."

"Go where?"

"Well, Trig Yamamura has connections in Honolulu. Or via people I know, we could probably finagle a start in New York, if you'd rather. The main point would be, stay away from here! For a few years anyhow, till you got your feet well planted."

Guido said in a low voice: "I've thought the same from time to time. But Bruce was the only one who ever got behind me and pushed, and he didn't have any such contacts."

He smiled. "Could be, Doc, that blue funk of yours is also situational. If I need to get away, maybe you need to settle down. Dig? Pipe, slippers, a wife and a lot of runny-nosed kids to worry about, instead of whatever dead thing it was that happened years ago."

"Let's quit the personal remarks," said Kintyre.

They drove on. The sea came into view, tumbling at the foot of steep yellowish cliffs. It was a cold, etched gray, under a gray sky. There was no clear horizon, sky and water ran together in mist. Guido had to slow down somewhat on the curves, but he managed a dangerous speed. Tires squealed and once he passed another car on a hill and avoided collision only by some inspired steering.

When they had left Berkeley more than an hour behind, he asked: "How far do you want to go, anyway?"

"Go on," said Kintyre.

"How come?"

Kintyre didn't answer.

At Half Moon Bay, the beach was empty and the clustered cabins forlorn; fog had closed in until you could not see past the breakers. It was clammy out there.

"Never liked the coast myself," said Guido. "She did — does, God damn it! She's queer for beach picnics. Likes to play volley ball and make sand castles."

Kintyre unclenched his fists.

"If we don't get her back," said Guido, almost matter-of-factly, "of course I can't leave home. The old lady won't have nobody left but me."

He crammed his foot on the gas. The car spurted ahead. The ground climbed again.

Presently they were on a deserted stretch. The land fell too abruptly to attract visitors: most places had no way down to the water. Sere brown hills lifted on the east side of the highway, trees huddled along them in clumps. The fog came streaming over the road.

"Now what?" said Guido. "It'll be socked in farther south."

"Continue," said Kintyre.

"Like hell!" Mutiny leaped on the dark snub face. "I've gone far enough. How d'you know they don't need us back in town?"

Kintyre felt his muscles congeal.

"What's the matter?" Guido stamped on the brakes. The car skidded to a halt.

Kintyre shuddered. The horror screamed, once, and drained from him. He knew remotely that it was not conquered — not yet — but his disintegrated self had coalesced for at least the time during which all of him would be needed.

He said, hearing his voice like another man's:

"Can you push this car back up to ninety going onward?"

"Huh?"

"I think I know where Corinna is."

Guido's hands slackened on the wheel. Suddenly they tensed again. The car growled from the shoulder and began to accumulate speed.

"I don't want to pile us up," said Guido, "but I guess I could average fifty. Where is she?"

"Do you know Point Perro?"

"I don't believe so."

"It's a little privately owned cove. Not far to go now. It's fenced off, posted, and there's nothing from the road to indicate it even has a beach. You couldn't find a lonelier spot in a day's driving."

Cloven air bawled past the windows. Guido squinted into thickening fog. He could only see a few yards ahead before the gray curtain fell; he had to imagine when the turns were coming up, and take them on two wheels. All at once Kintyre was terrified of an accident.

"I mentioned it to Clayton a couple of days ago," he said. The words came out one by one. "I seem to have forgotten that — down underneath, perhaps, I didn't want to admit to myself I'd given him any help — but I don't think it was coincidence I chose this route. Never mind. Clayton is an Easterner. His time out here has been spent entirely in the respectable sections of the Bay Area. Silenio and Larkin are complete strangers. How would they know where to take her, except some such randomly learned-about spot as this? At least, it's one chance for us. One chance!"

Guido said above the wind, the engine, and the wheels: "If you're right, Doc, it's even a good chance. An Easterner would drive a lot slower than me along this route, especially when they hit the fog. We might catch up to them."

"They've had hours," said Kintyre. "On the other hand, they had to meet each other too, and confer. They're not supermen, they would try to think of something, and argue about their plans, for a long time while they just drove aimlessly, surely not in this direction. We can hope."

"If they've done anything to her," said Guido, his face the mask of flayed Marsyas, "I myself will — "

"You'll let me off at Point Perro," said Kintyre. "Then burn up the motor getting to a phone. Don't waste time on any sheriff's office, call Berkeley headquarters direct. They can call the local authorities for you. It should actually be quicker that way."

"You, though," said Guido. "I can't leave you alone with them."

"Do you want to help Corinna, or do you want to get yourself sliced open for no purpose at all? You're a better driver, so you can get help sooner. I'll have a better chance of delaying matters down in the cove."

"I suppose so." Guido spoke it with difficulty.

"'One must therefore be a fox to recognize traps, and a lion to frighten wolves,'" recited Kintyre in Machiavelli's Italian. "'Those that wish to be only lions do not understand this.'"

Guido laughed shakily. "Modest fellow," he said.

Kintyre would have liked to clap his shoulder, but dared not. They were going seventy miles an hour on a winding road and it was becoming less visible each minute.

"Good for you," he said. "We'll salvage you yet." After another mile: "Or do you even need it any more?"

20

The fog had grown so dense that Kintyre knew his goal only by the car parked at the roadside. "Don't stop!" he cried, the moment it hove into view. "Brake easy. Let me out a hundred yards on." He began to open the door. "The nearest phone I remember is a gas station a few miles farther south. Don't raise your own posse and come back. They'd hear you and might shoot her first. Wait for the police. Good luck."

They rolled softly through a dripping gray swirl. Kintyre stepped from the car. Contact jarred in his feet. Almost, he fell, running alongside it in search of balance. Then the dark wet body slipped from him and was lost. He heard a muffled slam as Guido closed the door, the rising drone of speed, and now just his shoes thudding on pavement.

He stopped himself and jogged back. He was no track star, but he remembered to conserve his wind. The fog was moving with him, its eddies and streamers gave him the nightmare sense of a treadmill bound south. He could see the highway and something of the right-hand cliff that rose up and lost itself overhead. To his left there was nothing, world's edge and smoky endlessness. The air was chill.

Presently he regained the automobile. It was a new model, built for an impression of lowness and width; it sat and bared its teeth between blind headlights like some garish dinosaur defying the glaciers. Judas! Suppose this was only a harmless passer-by? But a signboard told him POINT PERRO, and who else would have come today? Kintyre tried the door. It wasn't locked. He eased it open to read the registration on the steering column.

Gerald R. Clayton. So. Kintyre felt his hands shaking. One more reassurance, before he went down the path. The dashboard thermometer showed the engine still warm. They hadn't been here long.

I do not wish for a God to help me, he thought. *But I wish I had one to thank.*

He filled his lungs and emptied them, filled and emptied them. Those were dank breaths, but they helped him ease up. He had three armed men to face; if he must also war with himself, it would be hopeless. Not that he felt any great conviction of winning. But — yes. He reached under the dash and yanked loose the ignition wires. After he was dead, that might delay their escape with Corinna.

He climbed the low barbed-wire fence. It guarded a jut of cliff maned with harsh yellow grass. You had to go to its very edge to see that there was a beach underneath. As he approached, he began to hear the surf. Incoming tide: breakers crashed among rocks, the water streamed down again with a roar, whirlpools gurgled in small grottoes. He did not think a human cry would be heard this far above.

When he came to the brink, he could just make out a sketch of jumbled crags and a laciness on the bull combers; then the rifted mist hid the sea from him again. There would be a highness to either side, the arms enclosing this inlet, but those were lost in the gray. He walked cautiously until he saw the path, a goat track plunging downward.

Its dirt was gritty under his feet. Despite himself, he loosed gravel showers now and again. After each he stopped, crouching and listening for voices. There were none: only the surf, snorting more loudly every time. The fog was his friend, could he have approached without it? Yes, he'd have found a way somehow, swum around a headland if he must, but the fog helped him. No proof of supernatural assistance, of course; this was a notoriously wet stretch of coast; however, he was advantaged thereby.

At the cliff's foot he stood among half-seen boulders and considered where his enemy might be. Not more than a hundred yards from him, but he had perhaps fifty feet of unclear vision. This pea soup was thickening by the minute. If the others arrived, say, twenty minutes ago, they would have been granted better visibility, could have selected a spot. Kintyre stretched his memory. The cliffs made a semicircular wall, with driftwood and great stones at its foot; the diameter was a narrow strip of sand, paralleled by a line of rocks. These latter were below high-water mark and would be drenched already. Kintyre could just glimpse the sleet-colored ocean breasting them. Okay. So his quarry was under the cliff. Was there some way to lure one of them out?

An idea came. It was hazardous, but no more so than blundering blind. And he was not afraid of what might happen to him. In a certain way, he had been given another chance to rescue Morna; he could not but take it.

Crouching in the rocks, he started to cough, as much like a sea lion's bark as he could manage. It was a bad imitation, but he dealt with pavement people. The noise went deep, wet, and ringing among the breakers.

"What's that?"

From the right! Kintyre fell on his stomach and began to eel his way over the rocks.

"A gahdam seal yet." Larkin's youthful whine. "Holy Moses, what a spot!"

"Better go see." It was an unfamiliar bass. Silenio.

"Ah, nuts, you go."

"You heard me, Terry," said Silenio.

"The girl knows this coast," said Clayton. Kintyre flowed over a bleached white tree trunk. It snagged his shirt, he had to stop and fumble for his liberty. And the fog talked and talked.

"It's just a seal, isn't it, Miss Lombardi?"

No answer.

"Silenio," said Clayton.

A tearing gasp: "Let go, you'll break my arm, let go!"

"I'm sorry to have to do this, Miss Lombardi," said Clayton. "But now that we've gotten settled here, such things will happen pretty continuously. Unless you cooperate. So to start with — that was a seal we heard barking, wasn't it?"

"Yes. *Oh!*"

"Go look, Terry," said Silenio.

Kintyre put his ear to the stones. He heard them rattle. If he could intercept Larkin, get him from behind without any noise....

He tried to judge whence the footsteps came. There were no more voices, no sound at all except Larkin and the sea. Kintyre followed, bent nearly double.

When he saw the vague shape, he changed course to intercept. Larkin was little more than a trench coat and a hat, fog-blurred. He was making no attempt to be silent, he slipped and stumbled, but his progress was quick. Kintyre decided he was going to get away, rose and sprinted the last few yards.

Larkin heard the hunter. He turned. "What — " Kintyre hit him. They went down together. Kintyre tried to get an arm around Larkin's throat. He didn't quite manage it. Larkin screamed.

That was a lost cause already. Kintyre wriggled free of threshing arms and legs, rolled away and bounded to his feet. Larkin was crawling to hands and knees. His face was a white blob with holes for eyes and mouth. He continued to scream.

Kintyre fled toward the sand. He heard Silenio curse. "What is it? What's going on out there?"

"It's a raid!" bawled Larkin. He reeled erect, the switchblade in one hand.

"Get back here!" said Silenio.

Kintyre whirled and threw himself prone. The sand was hard against his stomach. He could make out Larkin at the very edge of visibility, head weaving around. "Where did he go?" Larkin was crying. "Where is he?"

"Get back, I said, back here before I start shooting!" yelled Silenio.

Larkin groped a way toward the bodiless voice. Kintyre went on hands and feet this time, a quadruped rush. Larkin heard something and looked behind him. Kintyre went flat, simultaneously. Larkin faced back toward the cliff and resumed. Kintyre came after him again.

Three feet away, Kintyre stood up and leaped.

Larkin could not miss that. He spun on one heel, his knife already slicing. Kintyre moved in, presenting his left side, staying just out of reach. Larkin stepped forward. He was wary on the uncertain footing, too wary to be thrown hard. Kintyre feinted a blow with his left hand. Larkin slipped aside to avoid it. That took some of the rattlesnake speed off his striking blade. Kintyre's right hand chopped down, edge on, as he bent at the waist. The steel went half an inch past his belly. His hand connected with the arm behind. In that awkward stance it was not a blow of the real bone-cracking force, but Larkin moaned and went down on one knee.

Kintyre kicked at his neck. Larkin lowered his head and took the impact on the skull. This boy was good! It threw him onto his back, though. Kintyre circled for an opening. Larkin sat up, poised the knife in one hand, and threw it.

Kintyre felt a dull blow in his left biceps. He stared down. The knife stood in the muscle, blood was a red shout against skin and cloth. Larkin scrambled to his feet and pelted in the direction of Silenio's cries.

Kintyre knew little shock. Coolness at such moments was normal; he even had time to think that. The blood was simply oozing around the steel, no important vessel had been cut. He went after Larkin.

The boy slipped on a wet rock. There were shadows ahead, Clayton's lair? Kintyre sprang for him. To hell with defensive judo. Larkin had just gotten up. He heard the feet which followed, turned around and lifted his hands. "Help!" he shrieked.

"I'm coming!" cried Silenio in the gray.

Larkin flung himself into a clinch. His arms wrapped around Kintyre's waist with astonishing strength. Automatically, Kintyre's right arm went up to jam into his larynx. But Larkin's chin was down, guarding the throat. His right hand let go and reached after the knife in Kintyre's flesh.

Kintyre pressed a thumb into the boy's jugular. Larkin choked and pulled himself free. The knife came with him, in his grasp; blood runneled from the metal. He stepped in to rip. Kintyre's right hand traveled up. The heel of it struck Larkin at the root of the nose.

Larkin gurgled and flopped backward. His face was no longer quite human: the blow had driven his nasal bone into the brain. So much for him.

Silenio burst from cold clouds. He was a squat balding man with a round blue-cheeked face. There was an automatic in his hand. He looked a fractional second upon Kintyre and the body. Then he fired.

Kintyre was already running. He didn't hear the bullets, or even the ricochets, only the flat *smack! smack! smack!* as the gun went off behind him. He crouched low, zigzagging a little. A pistol is not a very accurate weapon. When he felt sand under his feet again, he looked back. Nothing but fog. He heard Clayton and Silenio calling to each other.

He glanced down at his wounded arm. It bled merrily. He flexed the fingers, tested their resistance to pressure: good, nothing had been severed which a few stitches wouldn't heal. But until he got the stitches, if ever, he had an arm and a half at best.

And Clayton and Silenio were still holding Corinna. It wouldn't take them long to think of making a hostage of her.

Kintyre hurried to the base of the cliff and went along it as quietly as he could. A weapon, how about throwing stones, no, they all seemed too large or too small. Bare hands were limited by the reach of an arm. Passing a log, he stopped to feel after clubs. He found a broken-off branch, four feet long and not very crooked. It had a narrow end, almost a point. Salt water and weather had turned it bone-white, iron-hard.

Kintyre followed the cliff. When he heard them talking again, he went with his back flat against it. Total silence would be his one chance, when he got into seeing range; they mightn't look his way.

They sat behind a log, a yard or two from the precipice. Clayton was huddled into a topcoat, hands in pockets, squatting wretchedly on a flat boulder. Silenio stood up, sentrylike, the gun in his hand.

Corinna sat facing Clayton. Her arms were free; a rope lashed her ankles. The long hair was heavy with dampness. She didn't seem to have been injured yet, except for that one short episode —

"It could only have been Kintyre," Clayton was saying. "And alone. Otherwise this beach would be solid with police."

"He may have the whole force on its way here," grumbled Silenio.

"That's possible. I think we had better get going. But remember, it's a single man. If you can nail him, we're safe."

Clayton stooped and began to untie Corinna. "I'm sorry about this," he said.

"Like hell you are!" she spat. Even now, Kintyre must grin at her rage, it was so much Corinna.

"As you like," shrugged Clayton.

"Why are you doing this?" she asked, almost with wonder.

Sudden pain sharpened Clayton's voice: "I've got three children. They'd be dragged down with me. The mud would stick to them all their lives. No!"

Kintyre glided forward. Corinna spied him over Clayton's shoulder. Through the watery air he saw her lips part. She cocked her head and looked out at sea. "What was that?" she exclaimed.

Clayton and Silenio turned wholly from Kintyre. He made the last few yards in a rush.

Silenio whipped around. Kintyre was almost upon him. He raised the gun. Kintyre thrust with his stick. It was ill-balanced, but he had fenced for many years. He got Silenio's hand and knocked it around. The gun went off with a crack; stone and lead spurted. Kintyre jabbed Silenio in the stomach. Silenio fell to his knees. He still had the gun. Kintyre snapped the point of his stick to the back of his enemy's hand and bore down. Bones parted; the stick went through, into the sand.

Silenio howled and tried to pull it loose. From the edge of his eye, Kintyre glimpsed Clayton's bulky frame launched at him. He let go the stick and caught an extended arm. He heaved Clayton over his shoulder and onto the rocks.

Silenio freed himself and scrabbled for the automatic. Kintyre put his foot on it. Silenio rose and threw himself at his opponent. The weight struck Kintyre's left biceps. Agony went like lightning. He staggered back, holding the arm.

The man from Chicago laughed. He picked up the gun, awkwardly left-handed, and fired.

And missed. Kintyre recovered himself, moving in again. Another shot went off nearly in his face. Another miss. There wouldn't be a third, he knew. He snatched up the stick. Silenio backed off, grinning with hatred. He steadied his left hand with the wounded right and took careful aim.

Kintyre lunged. It was a swordsman's movement, more leap than stride, with all his mass behind it. He took Silenio in the throat.

Silenio dropped the gun, clawed at the stick, and began to fold up. He tried to call out, but could only say blood. He sat down in a dazed way, plucked at his neck, and bled to death.

Kintyre had no time to notice it. He saw Clayton coming back. It did not seem possible Clayton could still move; the left side of his face was one giant bruise, the cheek flayed. Kintyre groped after the gun. Where was it?

Clayton advanced with a rush. He fell the last six feet. Raising his head and his arm, he showed metal in the hand. "Got it!" he said.

Kintyre pounced on him. They rolled over, kneeing and gouging. Clayton hammered a fist on Kintyre's hurt. The grasp on him loosened. Clayton writhed free, got up and ran. The fog whirled him from sight.

Kintyre pulled himself to hands and knees. Blood dripped from his wounds, bright little puddles formed on the ice-gray stones. His head tolled.

Hands fell gently upon him. He sat back, leaning into the circle of her arms. Her hair brushed his face. "You came," she said.

"Are you hurt?" he asked.

"No. There wasn't time. Oh, your poor arm!"

"Can you make some kind of bandage for it? My tee shirt will do."

"It isn't sterile. No, there are antibiotics these days, thank God for that." She pulled the garment over his head, sawed the seams across on an edged stone, and ripped it up. He noticed that her dress was gray. When she looked directly at him, her eyes and blonde hair were the only color in his world.

"Thank God for you," she added.

Her hands were deft, fashioning a compress and binding it in place. He kept his head toward the sea, listening. "What is it?" she asked.

"Clayton. Where did he go?"

"Wouldn't he try to escape?"

"If so, fine. I sabotaged his car. Or even if he gets it going, he'll never make it out of this state. But I'm afraid he realizes as much himself."

She knelt behind him, where he sat on the ground regaining his breath, and laid a hand in his hair. She asked steadily: "What will he do?"

"In his place," said Kintyre, "I'd come back and kill us. He should have done that when he broke free of me, he had the gun. But of course he was half stunned. Now that he's had a little time to think the situation over — yes. If he got rid of us, there'd be no witnesses to prove he hadn't also been kidnaped and was the single fortunate survivor. The kind of lawyers he can afford would have at least a chance to brazen out that yarn."

He stood up. "Fade back along the cliff, away from the path," he said. "Find yourself a sheltered spot and hunker down in it. If you need help, scream."

"You?" For the first time he heard fear. She stood up, and trembled.

"As I said, he has a gun and he will probably be stalking us, if he hasn't started yet," Kintyre answered. "I'd better forestall that."

She considered him with a somehow old look.

"All right," she said. "There is no other way. Christ guard you."

She reached up and kissed him, a brief light contact, and walked away.

Kintyre stood thinking of a certain letter. It had been written by Machiavelli from the farm at San Casciano, after he had gone there disgraced, tortured, and exiled, with all his work fallen, to dust. He wrote a friend:

"All my life I have behaved as I chose in love affairs. I let love do as it likes with me, I have followed it over hill and over vale, through fields, through woods, and after all I think I have done better than if I had avoided it."

You needed a certain courage to be happy.

Kintyre turned and went toward the path. It was a starting point for his search; Clayton's instinct would have been to bolt. He made no effort to be still. A snap shot in the fog wouldn't hit him, except by chance, and his racket would draw attention from Corinna.

Nevertheless, when the fire came, it was shocking. From the sea!

Kintyre whirled and padded toward the water. Clayton must have thought to circumvent him, wade out and around till he struck the cliff. Or perhaps he figured to hide among the rocks and — No matter. It was necessary to get him.

The tide was coming in heavily now. Kintyre saw how the sand gleamed, even in this sunless air, and then how it was whelmed in foam. Spray beat his face; he heard a hollow sucking roar among the stones. Where was Clayton?

Out in the surf, it tongued flame. He saw the beach furrowed beside him. So — crouched on a rock, approachable only through the water! Kintyre ran along the shore, trying to get out of visual range before a bullet smote him. The pursuing shots had a muffled sound.

He entered the water. It was savagely cold. It pulled at his ankles, sand shifted under the tidal drag. How deep was it where Clayton laired? Not over a man's height: Clayton was planning to get Corinna also, he'd have to come back ashore without wetting his gun too much. Not that a brief soak would disable a well-oiled automatic. But he would first lure Kintyre to him, if he could. A man struggling through chest-deep turbulence ought to make an easy target.

Kintyre strained eyes into the fog. He could just see the fortress rock as a shadow, fifteen feet high at the peak, forty feet long, Gibraltar-shaped. Breakers hurled against its seaward flank. This was a rapidly sloping bottom. The depth on Clayton's side was hardly over four feet, but it might be ten at the western end of the rock.

Kintyre waded straight out until a wave hit him in the face. He kicked off his shoes and swam.

His bad arm gave him saw-toothed pain and reddened the water. He used his right, a side stroke. The undertow grabbed him and yanked him outward. He wrestled to stay afloat. A comber went over him. Briefly he was in a remembered darkness.

He drank salt fear, threshed to the wave's top, and spun down into the trough behind it. A chill seething had him. It bawled in his ears. He knew himself empty of strength and hope.

The sea battered itself upon the earth, recoiled, laughed, and reared back to gallop in again. It was like the beating of a maul. A ship, a man, a girl could be crunched between wave and stone until ribs broke across. Kintyre strangled in a noisy wild night. He was spewed up again for a moment, scornfully. Spray sheeted in his face. The cold drained him, he could feel how warmth ran out. The sea rolled him over and toned in his skull.

Somehow you could swim, he thought. It was only to keep going. Though all the world were smashed on a reef, you could keep going. And there could be victory.

He saw the rock face shine before him. The waves pounded him against its roughness. Fog smoked in his eyes. He let the sea upbear him, and took its anger, while he fumbled about. His fingers closed on something, a handhold. His toes sought beneath the surface.

He pulled himself out.

For a little while he lay on the sloping stone back. The tide covered his feet. Life returned in some measure. He sighed and began to climb.

At the peak he looked over. Clayton sat on a small ledge, four sheer yards below him. The ruddy hair hung dark, there was blood matting one side of the long narrow head. Clayton's gun wove about in a seeking fashion, aimed toward shore and then down again. Once he jerked, making an odd little whimper like a lost child, and fired. The sound was flat, nearly lost among rumbling tides.

A twelve-foot jump could easily miss that tiny projection — and once fallen into the water below, Kintyre would be Clayton's. But so he would be if he tried to crawl down.

He made his estimates, poised, and sprang.

His feet struck Clayton between the shoulders. They went over together. It spouted where they hit. A wave swung in from the ocean and climbed the rock in one white burst.

Kintyre came up. He stood in four feet of water. Clayton was just arising. Somehow, incredibly, he still had the gun. It lifted, at point-blank range.

Kintyre's left arm found the power to chop down. The gun was knocked loose. The sea ate it. Kintyre laid his good hand upon Clayton. Enough.